THEN WHY NOT EVERY MAN?

KIT PRATE

WOLFPACK PUBLISHING
— EST 2013 —

WOLFPACK
PUBLISHING
— EST 2013 —

Then Why Not Every Man?

Paperback Edition
Copyright © 2021 (As Revised) Kit Prate

Wolfpack Publishing
6032 Wheat Penny Avenue
Las Vegas, NV 89122

wolfpackpublishing.com

All rights reserved. No part of this book may be reproduced by any means without the prior written consent of the publisher, other than brief quotes for reviews.

This book is a work of fiction. Any references to historical events, real people or real places are used fictitiously. Other names, characters, places and events are products of the author's imagination, and any resemblance to actual events, places or persons, living or dead, is entirely coincidental.

Paperback ISBN 978-1-64734-196-1
eBook ISBN 978-1-64734-195-4

THEN WHY NOT EVERY MAN?

For the girls, unto the fourth generation, by blood and by marriage; with much love from GP

Love is eternal…

Chapter 1

_____

They were singing as they worked, the field niggers that had been plaguing and badgering the boy from the first day he had been brought back to the plantation. They had given him a new name then, one they called him in front of white man and slave alike: *Runaway, Runaway Fool.* And, white or black, they said it with the same ridicule, with the same mocking laughter.

The words of their song came to him, falling on ears that knew the hidden meaning in all their music. The others sang of their fruitless dreams of freedom, the songs he refused to sing, and yet he found hope in their plaintive, melancholy song. *Didn't my Lord deliver, Daniel, deliver Daniel* they wailed, the chopping sounds of their hoes beating a steady cadence to the melody. The boy found himself silently mouthing the next verse (he would not give those near him the satisfaction of yielding even a little to join in their singing), allowing the words to etch themselves into the depths of his soul. *He delivered Daniel from the lion's den*, his heart sang, *and Jonah from the belly of the whale; the Hebrew children from the fiery furnace; then why not every man?* He repeated the last aloud, suddenly not caring who heard.

The boy's hoe chopped even more deeply now, his mind working and filled with the hope of the very young. All of his life, he had heard the marvelous assurances of the white man's God. Salvation and the promises of deliverance and the rewards that were stored in Heaven for those free of sin.

Sin. The word had always been a puzzle to him. He knew of no sin he was guilty of unless it was the sin of his blackness, his mahogany-colored skin the white preacher had called the mark of Cain. But how could there be guilt — *how could there be sin* — where there had been no choice?

From his first memory, he had hated his blackness. He had been trained from birth to be ashamed of what he was, to accept the fact that his color made him something less than human. No true man was bought and sold like a piece of livestock, offered up at auction to the highest bidders while white groping hands reached out to test his muscles, his teeth, to probe at his privates. White men treated their horses and cattle with greater concern, even a degree of affection. But their niggers? They were divided into lots, their worth judged by their age and the services they could render. The women were classed as domestics, field hands, breeders, nannies, and the very young as attractive as playthings.

It was not too much different for the men. His last owner had chosen him when he was only ten when his features were as fine and as delicate as an adolescent girl. For the five years he had been forced to remain with the man, he had known the hell and degradation of serving as a houseboy, passed around by the man and his sons, and on occasion, to their many guests.

The rage was still with him, the memory of the long nights in the old place gnawing at his very soul. It pounded in his ears with ever heightening intensity; the *whoosh* one with the increasing beat of his heart. Even the tempo of his hoeing had changed as his anger mounted; the methodic rise and fall of the tool somehow vicious; and it was a long time before he realized he was no longer chopping at the weeds in rhythm with the singing.

In fact, the melodic chanting of the other field hands had stopped. The silence was ominous, as dark and as fearsome as the massive shadow that suddenly loomed massive beside him; a dark wraith rising from the depths of Hell.

"Boy!" The voice boomed across the quiet. "Just what the hell you think you're doin', nigger?" The man swung at him, his fist landing solidly against the side of the youth's bent head. "That's *corn,* you ignorant, black bastard! You done chopped three hills of corn, clean down to the roots!!"

Runaway's head lowered even further and he desperately looked as far aside as his bowed head would allow. The others had gone back to their hoeing, their backs turned to what they knew was inevitable. The boy braced himself as he watched the overseer's massive silhouette pull the wooden ax handle from his belt and raise it above his head. Then, from within the youth, from the depth of his very being, came a long, almost animal cry of rage; a rage that had been too long denied. The overseer backed up, a look of surprise and fear draining the color from his sun-red face and neck.

Runaway liked what he saw in the white man's face. For the first time in his life, he had instilled fear in another; fear and desperation. The boy smiled. He watched as the field boss retreated a full pace, the man's eyes searching the faces behind the youth, looking for someone — anyone

— who would help him.

Without any conscious thought, Runaway raised his hoe and with one blow, severed the artery that stood out raised and blue against the whiteness of the overseer's neck.

The youth ran, the last sound in his ears the slow coughing gurgle that had accompanied the man's desperate, but failed, attempt to cry out. Fear prompted the speed with which the boy moved across the rows of spring-green corn. He knew that one of the field hands would be on their way to the main house for help, and soon — so very soon — the paddy rollers would be after him.

He sprinted like a young colt, moving across the tilled field toward the only hope for escape, welcoming the cold wet of the mud as he reached the river's edge. The going was harder now and he knew there would be a considerable distance to go before he would reach a place where the water would be deep enough to swim. The thought spurred him onward, his gaze on the far horizon. He was in the river now, the ankle-deep water finally giving way to sunlit pools that warmed his calves and then his thighs. Behind him, above the splash of the water, he could already hear the faint baying of the hounds. The sound grew, the pack of dogs growing more frenzied when they reached the fallen field boss, the fresh scent of human blood exciting the animals and increasing the intensity of the cries.

He plunged into the river's dark depths, seeking refuge among the thick water reeds and cattails. He could run no more and, not caring, sunk down into the cold muck, his breath coming in short gasps that burned his lungs and shook his entire body. The baying of the dogs was closer and they were searching out his scent at the water's edge. Runaway could hear the cursing of the dog handlers and then the noise of the others. There were men on horseback, urging their animals into the water as they slashed at the cattails with their rifle butts.

The boy pressed his body against the reddish mud, praying fervently to any god who might be listening that he not be found. He had killed a white man, but life as it had been and would be was still better than dying.

***

It was dark when the boy woke from his deep slumber. He was immediately aware of the wet and the cold even before he realized he was alive and — more strangely — alone. His last clear memory was of the closeness of the dogs and the desperate prayers he had aimed at the heavens. It was as if he had become invisible as if his body had become one with the earth and the water.

He realized now he had fainted. Suddenly ashamed, he stood up, the cold of the night air making a halo of mist about him as it crept into his skin and robbed his body of its warmth. He knew that he had to get out of the river and was filled with the fear of what might await him on the dry land so close to where he had entered the water. The river was his only real hope for escape and he steeled himself against the cold as he began the tedious chore of wading.

Knowing that the river ran a southeasterly course, he moved against the current. As long as he moved against the flow, he would be going north, north toward the Promised Land. Above him, a full moon shone brightly, almost as if mocking him with its bright yellow glow. *Why*, he wondered, *did the sun give heat and the moon not?* They both shone down from the same heaven, both glimmered with the same yellow light. He shook his head. Perhaps the sun was closer, he reasoned; it appeared so. There had been a time when he cursed the sun for too much heat just as he was now cursing the moon for too little.

His body began to respond to the efforts of his labored wading. The ill-fitting clothes that hung on his body were still wet but seemed less cold to him. He knew now what he must do. He would walk the river during the nights and during the days, he would burrow into its banks and occasional islands like the animal the white men had taught him to be. He laughed at that thought, a bitter, angry laughter not unlike the one that had escaped him when he had killed the field boss. Somewhere in the darkness, a night bird mocked him.

His journey continued in much the same way for the following two days. The cold no longer mattered. What he felt now was the hollowness that came with the intense hunger of a body already ravaged by years of meager diet. He felt as though each breath he took drew his stomach ever closer to his backbone and death by starvation.

On the morning of the third day, he burrowed into the sun-warmed sand of a small island mid river, not caring if he ever woke up from his sleep or not. For what it was worth, he had tasted the mythical freedom he had coveted for as long as he could remember and found that it did not fill his belly or warm his back.

His digging was almost mechanical, done in the fashion he had labored in the fields. His head ached and the long muscles in his legs were a series of cramps that reached from his hips and extended beyond his toes. He had suffered beatings that had not caused him as much pain and after those beatings had enjoyed the luxury of hating those who had abused him. Now there was no one to blame but himself and in his anger, he dug at the sand even harder.

His fingers closed around something warm, round and

fragile. He felt a flood of sticky warmth against his palm and when he withdrew his hand, it was covered with the rich yellow of yolk. The laughter that came now was filled with the richness of a joy that was purified by tears not of pain, but of gratitude. The boy explored the sandy nest carefully, piling the eggs gently beside him. The shallow pit yielded eleven eggs and the boy punctured each in turn, sucking them dry. As his hunger was satisfied, the aches of his body began to subside, and he began thinking more clearly. He could not risk a fire, even after the passage of days and miles, but if one turtle was laying eggs now, there would be others. And he would remember to look for them.

Sleep came easily, the small burrow he had made in the sand providing him warmth, while the long grass concealed him. He slept soundly, well into the night, and when he awoke, the sky above him was black as any he remembered and filled with shimmering blue-white stars more beautiful than the gems that arrayed the ball gown of any highborn lady. He stood up, spreading his arms to the heavens. They were his; all of them, and no thief could take them. *No white man could ever take them.*

The water seemed colder when he entered it and the current swifter. The river had widened considerably as he trekked north and he knew it would not be much longer before he was in country that would be strange to him, country that would be foreign and hostile. The old fears began to gnaw at him. He knew nothing of the world beyond the plantations. In his entire life, he had been no more than fifty miles from the place where he had been born. Even in the many times he had been sold, it was never more than a long half-day ride to the next plantation, to his next prison.

Freedom was in the North. He had heard that in the cabins and at the Sunday meetings. But where was North?

How far? How many days? There were supposed to be friendly white men there, but how did you know which one? And what white man would be a friend to a runaway nigger who had killed one of their own? He was sweating now. He was afraid, afraid as he had never been in his short life. So afraid that he felt a warm trickle against his inner thigh as he wet himself.

What if freedom was just a lie? He had never known a slave who had made it to freedom. *What if all the slaves he had heard talking about freedom had just been telling stories; had told him all these things just to see if he was foolish enough to believe?* He did know slaves who had tried to run; slaves who had been caught and brought back, broken and bleeding. Hobbled. Castrated. *What if the ones he thought had made it to freedom had been killed?* The bosses never talked about them, they only talked about the ones who had tried to run and had been brought back. *The ones that had been tortured and maimed.*

The doubts began to tear at him again. *What if North was nothing more than the Heaven the preacher and the old women talked about; and freedom nothing more than the wind? Heaven was where the good niggers went when they died, or so the others said.* A sobering thought struck the young man. *Maybe that was the only freedom for a nigger,* he reckoned, *death.*

Angered at his own ignorance, the boy waded out of the river. Something inside him — a growing voice — told him that all this suffering was for nothing; that no matter how far he walked, how hard he looked, he would never find any of the things he was seeking. He felt that he had as much chance of realizing any of his dreams as he had waking up one morning to find out he had turned white.

The rage was growing within him again; the rage and

the frustration that was feeding his fear and his doubts. He lifted his head in a need to vent his anger verbally and he screamed.

The scream ended as abruptly as it began. From beyond the thick brush, the youth sensed the acrid smell of fire. Instinctively, he dropped to the ground and began snake-crawling through the undergrowth and up a small rise.

Beyond him in a clearing, a big man lay on his side, facing away from Runaway and seemingly unaware that the boy was watching him. He was propped up on one elbow, staring into his campfire as though the only thing that mattered lay before him in the flames. Runaway stayed hidden in the thick swamp grass, watching the man and the occasional whiffs of white smoke that emanated from about his head. The man was smoking, the sweet smell of rum-soaked tobacco drifting with the wind. Runaway felt his empty stomach growl, the aroma of the rum and something else combining to remind him that he had not eaten.

The stranger threw his smoke into the fire, his back still to the thicket where the boy lay. "Might as well come in, child," he crooned. "Ain't no use you stayin' out there in the dark, freezin' your tail off and wishin' for a bit of old mister rabbit." He picked up the metal rod that had been suspended over the fire, holding up the impaled rabbit for inspection.

Runaway stood up, enticed by the smell of the meat. He was poised to run but his rumbling belly held him in place. "How, mister?" he asked softly. "How you know I was here?" The boy still had not moved.

The big man's laughter was soft, non-threatening. "I could feel it, boy. I can always feel it." The man rose up from his bedroll, stretching to his full height before turning to face the boy.

"Lord …." Runaway said the word without thinking. He had never seen such a big man or one so well-armed. There was a pistol shoved into the man's belt and a long knife strapped within easy reach on his left leg. The boy's eyes moved from the man to the horse that stood picketed beyond the fire, and back again to the man.

The man was black.

"It bothers you, boy?" The stranger took a single step forward, into the soft glow from the fire. "A nigger with a horse and a gun?" He took another step, moving toward Runaway, the smile coming too easily. He stopped when the boy took a step backward into the long grass.

Runaway studied the man, his mind trying to remember the stories he had heard about black men such as this. He knew that some niggers bought their freedom, but that meant cash money, a lot of cash money.

Or, he realized, *a special talent — skill — the white men needed.* "Slave catcher," he breathed. "*Slave catcher!!*" This time he screamed the words. He turned, intending to flee, only to have the man's big hand clutch at him.

"Don't make it hard on yourself, nigger," the other whispered. "Dead or alive, you're worth five hundred dollars to me." The man's fingers dug into the flesh on Runaway's shoulder. "Your master, he wants you bad, boy. You did a dumb thing, child. You killed yourself a white man!" The bounty man reached behind him, groping for the shackles he kept on his belt. He was smiling — sure of himself — and for one brief moment, he relaxed his hold on Runaway's boney shoulder.

Runaway jerked free from the man's grasp, turned, and ran into the thick brush. He could hear the slavecatcher behind him, the man swearing as his bulk made his pursuit of the boy difficult.

The youth ran towards the main channel of the river, praying he could make it into the water. He was a strong swimmer, one who had learned in the swamps and rivers that surrounded the farms where he lived. Once again, the water was his only hope.

The bounty man was behind Runaway, calling out; first, in mock friendliness, and then in vile curses and fierce threats. He was gaining on the boy, running at an angle with the water, his footing more secure on the dry ground.

Runaway felt the mud beneath his bare feet, and it slowed him. It was as if the muck were reaching out at him, clutching at him just as the slave catcher had grabbed at him. His chest ached with each stride as if the skin were two sizes too small for his rib cage, the mud clinging to his feet and giving him the sensation that he was wearing leg irons.

He was crying, as much from exhaustion as from the pain. It was as if the river — the water he had always considered his ally — had turned its forces against him. He could hear the slaver behind him, gaining ground and moving into the water. The quickening flow of the water-way was interrupted again and again by the steady plod of the huge man as he continued his pursuit.

There was a splash, followed by a sudden, unnatural sound as though the black bounty hunter had belly-flopped hard into the water. Runaway could not bring himself to look back, the river closing around his knees. Desperate, he plunged headfirst into the channel, pulled along with the current as the caked mud dissolved from his feet. And then, out of the darkness, it came. A long, piercing scream cut eerily into the black night, swelling above the deepening channel for what seemed a lifetime, then fading and dying into a foreboding silence. Only then did the boy stop swimming, treading water and fighting the undertow as he peered into the darkness behind him.

The big man was face down in the water, his shirt bloused out high above his back, his body bobbing and spinning with the now swirling current. The still form moved with the water, carried along until it lodged against a rock, suspended for a time, and then pulled free. The body drifted, hanging up against the rotting trunk of an uprooted tree, bobbing there for a time, pausing, and then moving on, closer and closer to the boy. It was as if — even in death — the hunter was still pursuing his human prey.

Runaway could not move. He kept treading water, watching the dead man with a macabre fascination as the body came closer. He could have reached out and touched the man's face.

The corpse hung up on an ancient piling, the water tugging at it until it was pulled up and into the current, the push of the water against the crumbling stone foundation flipping the body face upwards. The youth tried hard not to look into the bounty-man's face, into the dead, staring eyes. The water had washed the wound on the side of the man's head, a bloodless, gaping wound the size of a child's clenched fist. The dark skin was rolled back, exposing a thin layer of fat, yellow-white, against the smashed bone of the man's skull.

Runaway shoved himself away from the rocks, away from the grotesque thing that filled him with such fear when it lived. He began to swim back to the shore, his body warming as he moved through the water. The river had been true to him, as faithful to his needs as no man had ever been faithful. The water had destroyed his enemy and redeemed him. *Even more, it had provided him with the dead man's belongings.*

The boy's swim was more leisurely now, his strokes sure and deliberate. It was as if the river were washing away all the fear and for the first time in his young life he began to understand what he had never been able to comprehend before: this was the significance of baptism. To go to the water filled with fear and despair and to rise from its depths filled with unlimited hope and desire.

Chapter 2

The horse sensed the boy's uneasiness. The animal's massive head came up sharply, its ears coming forward and then going back again, tucked flat against the gelding's tousled mane. Neck stretched, the animal bared its teeth and raked the youth's forearm, a long trail of saliva marking the sudden welts that marred the boy's dark skin. Runaway stood his ground, clenching his teeth against the pain. Determined, he reached out, his left hand closing on the cheek strap as he drew close to the bay's left side.

Runaway had ridden before, many times. Bareback, mostly, aboard the broad-backed mules used for plowing, and on occasion — when he was smaller — on the padded surcingles used on the racing thoroughbreds.

But this animal was different. He had the look of a dray horse, thick-bodied and broad across the chest, built for endurance rather than speed. *So big,* he marveled, feeling suddenly small. He guessed at the animal's height. *Seventeen; maybe eighteen hands*, he reckoned. Reaching for the saddlebow with both hands, he squared his shoulders, the single, one-piece reins gathered in his left hand. The horse was skittish and Runaway moved cautiously, mindful of the animal's shod hooves and the damage the gelding could do to his bare feet.

He mounted, using the stirrup to hoist himself into the saddle. Settling himself, he kicked loose of the stirrups, gripping the horse's sides with his lower legs. The stirrups were too long, the metal irons a good six inches below Runaway's bare soles. He debated with himself, wondering if he should dismount and adjust the leather straps, shaking his head when he felt the gelding bunch under him. Keeping a firm hold on the reins, he nudged the horse in the sides. The bay hesitated, its ears busy. And then, mouthing the snaffle bit, the horse moved out.

Runaway exalted in his new-found mobility. He urged the big horse into a gentle lope, feeling the wind on his face, contentment in him as the moon-lit landscape slid by. The bay moved easily beneath him, his hooves cutting into the moist turf at the water's edge. Effortlessly, as if he carried no weight at all, the gelding continued at his ground-eating pace as he carried the boy farther and farther north.

The deceptive feeling of freedom gripped the youth, making him careless. He rode without regard to light or dark, content — bewitched — by the horse's seemingly tireless gait, the steady cadence of the animal's feet hypnotic. Night, illuminated by the full face of the moon, began to yield to the scarlet light of dawn. Runaway shouted a greeting to the sun and continued on.

***

There were two of them. White men, well-armed, mounted on near identical Morgans. They were on a bluff overlooking the point where the Tennessee Rive widens to flow into Kentucky Lake. The eldest of the two stood up in his stirrups, a brass telescope pressed against his right eye. He eased back into the saddle, the leather creaking beneath him as his weight shifted, and carefully closed the tri-sectioned spy glass to its reduced size. Half turning, he shoved the magnifier in his kit bag. "It's Boone's horse," he said softly, "but that's not Boone riding him." He scratched at the three-day growth of sun-silvered beard that sprouted from his chin.

"What the hell you mean, *it ain't Boone?*" The younger man moved his horse abreast of the other. He pointed his arm at the distant figure. "Even without that damned glass, I could see it was Boone's horse." He faced his brother, his neck red. "I tol' you that! Afore, when I seen him." He jabbed his finger at the object of their discussion, accentuating his words with a poke for each one. "Even a blind idgit kin see that's a nigger astride him!"

"Caleb," the older man said quietly, "even a sighted idiot can see that *that* darky…" he raked his brother with a long, cold stare, "…isn't Boone." He reached beneath his right knee, dismissing his half-brother and unsheathed the Sharps carbine that nested there. Without speaking, he kicked his horse into a trot, knowing that Caleb would follow. Silently, the two of them shadowed their unknowing quarry.

They kept up their quiet pursuit. Caleb muttered incessantly, his eyes alternating between his brother and their prey. They stayed above the boy, above and behind him. Watching, watching and waiting.

***

Runaway pulled his mount to a standstill, reaching out to finger the arched neck. He patted the animal, urging him into the shallow water along the shoreline. Then he leaned forward, allowing the animal to drink, hearing the loud sucking sound from deep inside the horse's throat. It fascinated him, how the animal could drink with his head so far below its belly. And then the boy laughed a rare thing for him, remembering a long-ago dare — a wager — with a nameless, faceless friend. They had bet it was impossible to drink water while standing on their heads. Runaway had taken the wager, not caring if he lost. And then he upended himself against the barn and took the cup.

That had been the hard part, he mused, remembering, *holding the cup.* But he had swallowed the water and with no difficulty at all.

He couldn't remember what he had won. It couldn't have been much, for neither he nor his friend had anything of real value to wager.

***

Elisha Montgomery signaled for his brother to stop, waving the man away from his horse and gesturing for him to dismount and keep his distance. The younger man did as he was bid and then changed his mind, snake-crawling to the place where Elisha lay belly down in the high grass that topped the windswept dunes. Caleb scrambled close to his brother's right shoulder, his mouth open as he started to speak.

"One word, Caleb," Elisha whispered, "One sound and I'll knock your teeth down your throat." It was no idle threat. He worked a cartridge from his belt and opened the Sharps' breech.

It was a long shot. Almost a thousand yards, he judged. He adjusted the slide bar on the raised rear sight and waited.

"You're gonna take down the horse," Caleb whispered, his eyes gleaming with a wicked, red fire. "Knock him down and then get the nigger!"

Elisha sighed, his concentration interrupted. Without looking back, he rammed his elbow into his brother's face, calculating the spot by the sound of the other's voice. It was a tempered blow, meant to punish, not maim. "I told you to stay quiet, Caleb." He paused, listening for the boy's muffled sobs. "I'm not going to kill that horse," he said, his voice quiet, patient, as if he were talking to a very small child. "I kill that horse; all I'll have is a saddle to tote and a pile of bones. But..." he closed one eye, his attention on the carbine again as he sighted the piece a second time, "...if that's the buck old Boone was trailing — dead or alive — that nigger's worth bounty. And it's a lot easier when he's dead." He waited until his quarry straightened in the saddle and fired.

**

There was no noise. Not at first. Runaway was aware of pain; sudden, hot pain that brought brilliant flashes of light. As if he had stared at the sun too long and been blinded. And then he heard the explosion and it echoed over and over in his throbbing ears.

The horse heard, too. Its head came straight up and back, the fist-sized bone between his ears with colliding with Runaway's chin as the youth tumbled forward. The gelding reared up, a sharp hurting in its head. Its burden shifted unnaturally, the boy's arm hung up in the reins, the momentum of the horse's sudden move and the boy's dead weight combining to create a force that threw the animal off balance. The gelding pawed at the air with its great hooves and then tumbled over backwards. Runaway was thrown clear, landing spread-eagled in the damp mud at the river's edge.

Elisha Montgomery was on his feet and mounted before the smoke from the Sharps had cleared. He sheathed the carbine and booted the Morgan into a run, shouting for his brother to follow. He gave no attention to the fallen youth, his mind on the big gelding. The animal was on its rear haunches now, struggling to rise. The bay regained his feet just as Montgomery broke through the long grass on the sun-soaked savannah.

The chase was brief, the big horse unable to outdistance the hardy little Morgan. Montgomery reached out, grabbing the reins. He pulled the animal to an abrupt halt, grinning as he inspected his prize. For a long time, he had coveted Boone's mount.

He led the animal back along the beach, keeping both horses at a walk. Up ahead, he could see Caleb, could see the crazy jig the youth was dancing around the fallen black.

"He ain't dead, 'Lisha!" The boy was still hopping up and down, pointing at the boy lying in the sand. "You creased him; clean as a 'coon!" He made a sweeping motion at the back of his own neck with his right hand.

The man nodded and dismounted. He laid a firm hand on his brother's shoulder, calming him. "You tend to the horses, Caleb," he ordered. He didn't wait for a response, just strode past the youth, his eyes on Runaway.

He knelt down, flipping the injured youth over, his fingers probing at the bleeding welt on the boy's neck. He had aimed for the head, a killing shot. This was luck, pure luck. Reaching out, he pinched the boy's arm, watching for some response, continuing to apply pressure until the boy convulsed and instinctively pulled away. Satisfied, he turned his attention to the youth's legs, proceeding in the same manner as before. *It could happen*, he thought, remembering his horse hunting days in Texas. You could crease an animal, simply stunning him, or cripple him for good. *Just a hair's breadth the wrong way*, he mused. He had killed more horses than he had caught that first year. He shrugged. There were always more horses in Texas. *Just like there were always more niggers in Tennessee.*

"What you goin' to do now, 'Lisha?" Caleb was beside his brother now. He reached out with his foot, toeing the still form that lay at his brother's feet.

Elisha stood up, considering the question. The reward for the fugitive they had been pursuing was small by comparison to what they usually took — a mere five hundred dollars. He thought about the advertisement he had been given by the owner: *Negro; young male, age Unknown. No identifying marks. To be hanged.*

It was, he realized, a waste. Digging into his pocket, he pulled out a paper bound wad of tobacco. Carefully, he trimmed off a chaw-sized plug, working it into a small brown ball between his thumb and forefinger. He pushed the dark brown wad into his mouth and worked it to the side of his jaw. "We're taking him home," he said finally, "back to Kentucky."

"To Pa?" Caleb's eyebrows raised, his expression hopeful.

Elisha shook his head. "To Uncle Perry's," he answered, thoughtful. *His uncle would reward him well for a proper buck like this*, he mused. *Real well, certainly better than his drunken father would do.*

***

They rode for more days then Runaway could count. North; always north. He could tell by the stars and it baffled him. He kept his mouth shut, watching the others the way he had always watched white men, covertly, without them knowing.

Runaway cared the least for the young one. The boy was about his size and age but not right in the head. He took his joy in tormenting things. Insects, frogs, the small animals his brother killed for food. Even the nesting turtles they found at the river's edge. He would pick them up and turn them over on their backs on the high, concave-shaped rocks dotting the shoreline, leaving them to die in the sun.

The older one was more of a puzzle. Runaway had a great deal of trouble understanding this one. He was a big man, almost as big as the slavecatcher and he had a quiet way of talking that made you listen. His manner and way of speaking were in stark contrast to his younger brother and it was obvious that he merely tolerated Caleb, at times behaving as if the younger man didn't really exist. He fed him, saw to it that his creature needs were met and that was all as if the youth were a tag-along hound Elisha kept for companionship but nothing more.

They camped, after yet another long day, Runaway — who had been shackled — building the fire for their evening meal as Caleb scavenged for more wood. He stared into the flames, his hand going to the scab at the back of his neck. Elisha had tended his wound, that first night, talking to him in the same quiet way he spoke to his brother. "You keep in mind, boy, that I could have killed you. And — if you try to run — I *will* kill you."

Runaway never doubted for a moment that the man

meant what he said. Every word.

There was no mention of Boone after that first night. Elisha had questioned Runaway, had pieced together the story about the thing that had happened at the river. But he asked nothing more from the youth. Not where he had come from, not what he had done. *Nothing*.

They had rabbit again, roasting the meat above the banked fire, rabbit and dried fruit. Runaway ate the same as the other two, equal shares of whatever game Elisha had taken down. They ate in silence, always in silence. And then he would clean up the litter from supper, wash up the dishes, and Elisha would tie him hand and foot. Caleb would walk into the woods then, to relieve himself and when he returned, he would kick out at whatever portion of Runaway's body that pleasured him.

Once, in the beginning, Runaway had cried out. When his brother questioned him, Caleb lied. "I tripped," he whined. And then, when Elisha looked away, Caleb kicked Runaway again, hard; the toe of his boot digging into the long muscle in the back of the boy's upper leg.

It would be the same again tonight, Runaway thought. *And it was.*

****

The plantation was bordered on three sides by water, by the upper Tennessee on the southwest, by a minor tributary of the Ohio on the northeast, and to the north, by the Ohio River itself. The land had been reclaimed from the river by a series of dikes and earthen dams. The silt-nourished soil was rich, a dark coffee brown.

The major field crop was corn, corn for the livestock and the Kentucky whiskey the old man drank and sold in abundance. The real crop, however — the cash crop — was human. Young women worked the fields, young women in the prime of their child-bearing years. These were slaves bred to provide more slaves. There were many babies on the brood farm, but few children beyond the toddler stage. As soon as they walked — as soon as they were weaned — they were taken from their mothers.

Taken, taught some rudimentary skill, and then sold.

Elisha was there, working for his maternal uncle. Overseer — surrogate owner, almost — and he moved among the slaves with a certainty and quiet grace that showed he was looking forward to the time when it was his, all his. He rode the fields astride the slave-catcher's big gelding, the pair of them immense giants always hovering on the horizon.

Runaway worked the fields as he had worked so many others. He was disliked by the other slaves because they knew why he had been brought to this place and mistrusted by them because of the continuing attention he drew from the field boss and Elisha. The white men watched him, knowing that if he had run once, he would run again. Or try.

So he labored, set apart from the others for reasons he didn't fully understand, the only thing that contented him the knowledge that Caleb, his tormentor, was gone. He had seen the fight between the two half-brothers, had seen and heard the hatred. Elisha, the firstborn in a union that had been doomed from the beginning — a marriage between his well-bred mother, and his loutish, ill-bred father — and Caleb, the bastard son of his father's white trash mistress.

Elisha had prevailed. Where Caleb had gone remained a mystery. Not that Runaway cared.

The corn was more than waist high now, the green

leaves spread wide beneath the hot sun. The earth was dry beneath Runaway's feet, dry and unmercifully hot. The sun scorched man and beast alike.

Runaway kept on at his hoeing. He had been on worse plantations, the larger ones in the deep south, with the acres and acres of cotton and cane. The weather there had been different, too, as well as the soil. This earth seemed to yield more than the other and the weather was more temperate.

The women working with Runaway began their long trek back along the rows to the shelter of the grove of trees at the field's southern edge. From the distance, Runaway could hear the fretful cry of the small babies, and he paused in his work, wiping his bare arm across his brow. He stared at the women, at the place where they had gone.

There was a long, hollowed out bench there, a manger of sorts. Tiny brown arms and legs waved bodiless from its depths as — one after the other — the hungry babies woke and cried out in hunger. The women tended to them, picking them up, jostling them in an attempt to quiet their cries. And then the angry wails began to abate, the women baring their full breasts to suckle the infants.

Runaway continued to watch. Very seldom had he witnessed any display of affection among his people. And yet, watching the women, he saw a tenderness that saddened and angered him. He had few real memories of his own mother and had no idea who had sired him. It was as if he had just simply come into being. Still, somewhere — in some faraway place, some faraway time — he, too, must have been held like this; nourished in this way.

"Boy."

The voice came to his softly, from behind, guarded but not entirely unfriendly. Runaway turned to face it. Elisha sat above him, his arms folded across the neck of his horse.

The man was smiling, a bemused, mocking smile. The boy met his gaze and just as quickly lowered his eyes. "Massa…" he mumbled.

Elisha was still smiling. He had observed the boy constantly in the past few months, impressed with the way the youngster could adapt from one circumstance to another. Like now, speaking in the monotone, broken English of the field slaves. Not at all the way he had surreptitiously heard the boy speak when he was questioning the house niggers, when he was as articulate as Uncle Perry's valet. The smile grew. "Can't hoe the corn and watch the women, boy," he scolded. He moved the big gelding closer, so close the horse's nose was on the boy's neck. Reaching out, he laid a big hand on the youth's head, forcing it up. "Your time will come, boy," he said, his eyes sweeping Runaway's lanky frame with the same look he would use judging a yearling thoroughbred. "You're a proper buck," he reasoned, still measuring the youngster. "Come time, we'll turn you loose with the hens," he nodded toward the women at Runaway's back. "You'll play rooster, help those biddies lay us some proper eggs, give us some proper chicks." He laughed then, turning loose of the young man and headed down the long rows.

Runaway turned back to his endless chore. He could hear the women as they returned, their banter stopping as they approached him. For some reason, their silence made him more aware of their presence than he had ever been before. One of them was beside him now and he could see the wet spot at the front of her camisole, the leakage from her prominent nipples. He cursed her, silently, and then moved ahead of her as his pace increased.

They were at the north end of the long row when it began to rain. The clouds had formed quickly, boiling across the summer sky. White, fluffy clouds at first, fast turning grey and then black. And then the sky opened up and it began to pour. Elisha moved among the women, cursing them, prodding them as he drove them toward the stand of trees that lined the wagon road at the end of the field.

There was hysteria among the women, a low murmur that began to grow as Elisha and two helpers forced them under the shelter of the dense tree limbs. Runaway was bewildered by their panic. There was no lightning, only the soft roll of distant thunder. And still, they stood there, rocking back and forth, first on one foot, and then the other, running in place. They were united in a tight knot, the nursing mothers and their eyes were all turned to the same place.

The trough.

Elisha ignored their pleadings. He and his men formed a man and horse barricade until the deluge stopped. The women broke then, moving with the first stream of sunlight that pierced the dispersing clouds. They were running, their bare feet trampling the earth and corn as they ran toward the opposite end of the field.

Runaway ran with them, for the first time understanding their fear. Unmindful of the men at their backs, they kept on, the only sound the sloughing of their feet against the tilled, muddy soil.

The long manger was filled with water. Runaway stopped but it was too late not to see. There was no sound from the children. They floated face down on top of the water. They were still, so damned still, bobbing like little brown corks at the end of a string of fishing lines.

A long, anguished cry tore from the women. Instinctively, each went to her own dead child, lifting the naked bodies from the still warm water. The wailing continued, softer now, a constant keening filled with the hopelessness of all the generations that had gone before, and for those that had just perished.

Elisha came, his men behind him. He surveyed the scene without one trace of emotion touching his tanned face and swore, his eyes narrowing. There were addition and subtraction going on behind those cold eyes, a reckoning of profit and loss. He was weighing the worth of the dead children like a fishmonger would tally a load of bad meat. He dismissed the loss as a temporary setback. "Get them out of here," he ordered, pointing to the dead infants. His voice rose and there was something in his tone that made the women listen. "Back to work!" He moved forward on the big horse, wielding the whip, using the shot-weighted handle like a club. The other men were on foot now, moving among the women, tearing the babies from them, and shoving the women towards the field.

One of the women began to laugh. It was a cold, terrifying sound that took the color from Elisha's face when he whirled to meet her scrutiny. There was a flash of recognition in the man's face — a brief flash, and then nothing. The woman, a tall, attractive Octoroon, held up her son, hoisting his limp body high above her head. "He's free, Elisha!" she shouted. "By God, at least *he's* free!!" She was still shouting when Elisha struck her.

The women returned to the fields, one by one, their quiet sobbing in cadence with their heavy step. Runaway followed after them, keeping his distance. He could hear Elisha's horse behind him and stepped aside.

"Looks like your time has come sooner then we figured," the man said, keeping the gelding in step with the boy. He was thinking of the ten dead slave children with his stockman's money mind as if the thing that had happened was no different than the loss of a single foal or calf. "Well, there's more to be had," he observed, as much to himself as to the youth that walked beside him. He laughed then and kicked the horse into a run, pursuing the women, herding them like so many cows.

The morning passed slowly. The women no longer cried and the silence was worse. It grew blacker as the wagon rumbled back into the field. *The same wagon that had carried their children to ...*

...where? The women had no way of knowing. Their anger increased, the rage growing as the weight of their full breasts brought a pain for which there would be no release. One by one, they dropped their hoes, slowly lowering themselves to the ground. Soon, only Runaway and one other — a young pregnant girl — continued with the hoeing.

Elisha moved among the women again, trying to prod them to their feet with his horse and whip. The women refused to move, covering their heads with their arms, accepting the man's abuse as they cowered closer and closer to the ground. Exasperated, the man stopped, his eyes on the midday sun. He cursed, knowing there would be no more work. Not this day, and not from these women.

He called out to his men, watching as the paddy-rollers that patrolled the fields joined them, hesitating as they waited for more sign from him. He stood up in his stirrups, nodding his head with exaggerated slowness, removing his hat as he waved the half-dozen men to him. His orders were hushed, terse. They were to go to the adjoining fields and cull them for other workers. The men dispersed, spurring their horses as they fanned out toward the lush fields that spread spoke-like from the rambling collection of buildings that glimmered white on the south-eastern horizon.

Elisha turned back to the women. His face was a dark red, mottled by the anger that burned in his chest. He was a man used to giving orders, giving orders and being obeyed. "Get in the wagon," he roared. "Now, goddamn you!" He dismounted, leading the horse, kicking the women to their feet, grabbing and shoving them toward the wagon. Ten of them, their faces one, set, grim, like chiseled obsidian. They clambered over the side of the wagon, mindful of the pools of water that marked the places where their children had lain.

Elisha tied the bay gelding off to the tailgate. He turned, his eyes probing the field. Still angry, he lifted his arm, pointing to Runaway. "You, too," he ordered. There would be no field work this afternoon, but they would earn their keep. *All of them.*

The boy as well. He glared at the youngster, calculating his age. *Sixteen,* he reckoned, *perhaps a bit older. No real flesh on him; not yet.* He nodded his approval. *In time,* he thought. The build was right, sturdy, resilient, almost classically proportioned. He waved the boy forward. The youth would need some teaching. He reached out, drawing the boy to him. "They grieve for their get," he said coldly. "We — you and I —" he poked Runaway's chest with a long finger, "will give them more." He jerked his thumb toward the wagon.

Runaway backed up a step. He could feel the women's eyes on him, their sudden hatred. He hesitated. It wasn't that he didn't feel the natural cravings of a boy becoming a man, but this...

...this was wrong. He shook his head, regretting the move as soon as it was made. Elisha grabbed him, one hand closing on the nape of his neck, the other digging into his

crotch. Bodily, the big man lifted him into the back of the wagon. He landed on his face, sick with the pain that tore at his groin, curled up like a naked grub as the women trod on his fingers and toes.

Elisha moved to the front of the wagon. He started to climb aboard, raising himself up from the ground, his foot on the hub of the front wheel.

The woman struck out at him — the same woman who had expressed elation at her child's death — her fist closed like a man's. A long year of field labor was behind the blow. She hit him squarely in the face, bloodying his nose; then hit him a second time, exactly between his eyes.

The man opened his mouth to speak and then slipped from sight. "Boy…" he called suddenly and the cry startled the team.

The mules bolted forward, dumping the women over. They regained their feet quickly, exchanging terrified glances as the man's voice rose in a sudden scream.

Runaway scrambled to the driver's seat and set the brake. He turned, staring down at the ground, at the man lying beside the wagon. It had happened so fast, so damned fast.

Elisha's face had drained of all natural color, his skin ash white. His breathing was labored and he stared up at the brown faces that hovered above him. One by one they disappeared, the wagon creaking as they disembarked. Only the boy and the woman remained. Montgomery fought to keep his wits, fought the pain that flowed through him in great waves. He saw the woman smile, misreading the expression, failing to see what lay behind the green-flecked eyes. "Charlotte…" he said softly, beckoning her with his good arm.

"My son, Elisha," she answered, "*Our son.*" Her words drifted off into nothingness. A single tear formed and traced a small thin line down her dust-filled cheek. She wiped it away. And then she spat on the man.

Runaway dropped to the ground. He was alone beside Montgomery, the women standing together in a small clutch behind the wagon. They were whispering, their voices argumentative. The youth turned his eyes to the white man.

Montgomery lay pinioned to the ground, his right arm beneath the heavy, iron-banded front wheel. There was blood, a great deal of blood. Pieces of bone had punctured the flesh above his elbow. He nodded at the arm. "Move the wagon, boy," he ordered softly. There was no plea in his words, no sign of weakness and for a fleeting moment, Runaway admired his courage.

But only for a brief moment. And then the youth shook his head. "No," he said, remembering the drowned children. *Elisha's cast-off son.* "No," he repeated, this time with more certainty.

Elisha blanched, his skin growing paler. "Please," he struggled to turn, grabbing at his torn arm. "For the love of God, help me!"

Runaway was already walking toward the women, his back to the man. *For the love of God…* The words echoed in his mind and he rejected them. There was no love of God, not in this place. "The river," he said, pointing behind the women to the broad expanse of water at their backs. "We have to cross the river."

The women stared at him. In the weeks he had been with them, he had never said anything more than 'yes' or 'no'. He came towards them, his pace increasing as they stepped aside. Just like the last time he ran, he headed toward the water, into the water.

And — without looking back — the women followed him.

Chapter 3

They made the crossing without taking the time to search for a suitable ford. Several feet from shore, the stagnant water remained only knee deep. Then, gradually, the murky waters began to deepen, the current intensifying. Several of the women began to weep, their voices lifting in a strange, primal litany as the others joined in. Runaway turned, watching them. The river reached above his waist now, and he could feel the sandy bottom being tugged away from his feet by the undertow.

The others were holding back, far back. *They can't swim*, he realized. He faced the women and then turned away from them to gaze at the far shoreline. Steeling himself, he looked back at the ragged band of women that waded behind him. He shook his head. With slow purpose, he lowered himself into the water. And then he began to swim.

He did not look back. He could hear the noise of the few women who followed him, could hear them sloshing through the river on both sides of him, behind him. He kept his eyes on the far shore.

There was a soft sound at Runaway's left shoulder, the moist warmth of someone's breath on his wet shirt and then the brief, clinging touch of someone's fingers. Then the breathing noises again, like the flutter of a barn swallow's wings when it approaches its nest. Soft, barely audible above the river. And then the hand slipped away and the sound was gone.

In his mind, Runaway marked the sound of the others that were swimming with him. There was one less now, one less labored sound of painful breathing, the rush of air gasping above the water.

Mid-river, the current began to carry them, holding them back from the opposite shoreline. And then, gradually, they began to gain again, the river narrowing, the water dotted with small sandbars that poked up from the deep green depths. They paused at the miniature islands, drawing themselves up out of the water just long enough to rest their arms and lungs.

They rested without speaking, without looking at each other. Their labored breathing slowly returned to normal, and — one by one — slipped back into the river to begin again.

The sun had dropped behind the trees when they reached a point in the river where they could feel the silt-rich bottom slick and warm between their toes. Eventually, the fine silt yielded to the pebble-studded sand of off-shore bedding. They rose up and began wading, heading into the long cattails that lined the beaches at the shallows.

Runaway glanced over his shoulder. *Four*, he counted silently. Of the ten women who had begun the crossing, only four remained.

They huddled in the sand, the women sitting with their knees drawn up to the heaving chests, their heads buried in the wet heaviness of the homespun skirts. Only the light-skinned Octoroon remained on her feet, withdrawn from the others, her gaze on the far shoreline. The drawn look was still on her, emptiness in her green eyes. She lifted her shoulders in one great sigh, clinging to herself for a time, slowly shaking her head. Runaway moved across the beach, standing beside her, intimidated by her unusual height and straight-backed bearing. "Three years," she said cryptically, acknowledging the boy's presence without looking at him. She nodded at the opposite bank. "For three years, I lived with Elisha. In his house," she said the words as if they should have some special significance. "I was his … woman," she breathed, her voice soft. She repeated the words, whispering them. "*His woman.*"

"And then he brought me here."

Runaway nodded without really understanding. He stared back at the other women for a time and then returned his eyes to the woman. "We have to get them on their feet," he said quietly. "We have to get them moving."

The woman raised an eyebrow, studying the youth. She had never hidden the fact that — as the Octoroon offspring of a white man and a Quadroon — her childhood had been genteel, almost privileged. *But this one…* He was full of secrets. She studied him, a small smile turning up one corner of her mouth. "Uppity nigger, aren't you?" she asked, watching his eyes.

Runaway met her gaze — returned it — his brown eyes burning with an anger that he fought back into the pit of his churning belly. "No more than you, woman," he retorted, raking her with his eyes.

"Then there is no need for any pretense, is there?" The woman's anger added an edge to her words, her tone matching the others. "Can you read?" she asked suddenly.

The question startled the boy and the surprise showed in his face. He thought for a time, debating if he should answer her truthfully. "I can read," he said finally.

The woman nodded her head. "My name is Charlotte," she said quietly. "Charlotte Bouvier." She took pains pronouncing the last, drawing the word out, accenting it: *Boo-vee-a.* "My father was Old World French and my mother a bright, a quadroon.

"His wife's maid," she finished, bitterness in her words. She stared at her arms, her pale skin. "She was a slave and that made me a slave."

"And Elisha?" The words tumbled out from the boy before he could stop them.

The woman laughed, a cold laughter filled with self-ridicule. "He loved me," she answered. "Moved me into his father's house and told me that if I lived with him, he would buy my freedom." She was silent, her face grim. "I would have lived with any man who promised me freedom." The self-scorn in her voice was replaced by an intense fervor that stoked a bright fire behind her pale eyes. "He moved me here, to his uncle's place, after the boy was born," she continued. "Gave me a son..." she raised her arms in a gesture of futile resignation; "...and then he had two slaves that were his own." Her face changed, becoming hard again. "He has no more," she said firmly. "Not now." It was as if she were in a trance, speaking as if to herself. She beat a knotted fist softly against her belly. "And he'll not have this one..." she promised.

Runaway studied the woman, wondering at her meaning. He dismissed the thought, his mind working. They could not stay in this place. "Get them on their feet," he ordered quietly, pulling at the woman's arm. When she hesitated, he released his hold. "Please." He turned from her then and began walking. North.

Soon, behind him, he could hear the soft plodding of bare feet, and the swish of the still wet dresses against the swamp grass.

***

For three days, Elisha Montgomery lay teetering between life and the great darkness that threatened to swallow him up forever. He hung on, calling out in his delirium, first for the woman and then — once — for the boy. His fever worsened and he felt himself melting like a wax doll. Voices came to him, came and faded and for a time he thought he heard the gnawing of rats. Close, so close that it seemed that they were on the bed next to him, crawling on him. He screamed then and was devoured by the darkness, lapsing into a long period of unconsciousness. But even then his mind would not be still. He could feel the pain, the excruciating pain in his mutilated arm and the gnawing sound continued to haunt him.

It was two weeks before he regained his senses, the bright light of a morning sun blue-white across his eyes. There was a terrible itching in the palm of his right hand, in his fingers. Without thinking, he reached across his chest with his left hand, intending to scratch the fingers of his right hand.

It wasn't there. *His right hand was not there!!* He rose up, beating at the empty blanket at his right side, his left fist moving farther and farther up the barren, crumpled covering to the place near his shoulder where he found the stub. He began to curse, vile, angry curses pouring from deep within him as his chest swelled with anger. Anger and hate.

For the boy that had refused to help him. Even more, for the woman who had maimed him, betrayed him, and left him to die.

***

They had continued their long trek up the west bank of the Wabash River, Runaway, Charlotte, the other women. They hid during the long days, resuming their travel at night.

Runaway provided their food, scavenging the small farms as they wandered, taking only what they could eat from the vegetable plots, occasionally stealing a chicken to supplement their otherwise meatless diet.

And then, in a small rural area north of the Patoka River, they were caught. A farmer took them, at the edge of his small garden plot, a small, bandy-legged man carrying a large, impressive shotgun. Without a word, he herded them back to his house, back to his barn.

That evening, he fed them, his wife and their stair-step children carrying pots of cooked food and herb tea into a narrow, secret room behind the great stacks of hay.

Charlotte spoke with the man, while they were eating. She used the dialect of the Deep South, feigning an ignorance that prompted the man to talk to her as if she were a very small child.

Later, once they had eaten and the man and his family had returned to their house, she sought out Runaway. She beckoned to him, leading him to the far corner of the room, to the place where he had made a thin straw pallet. "This is a station," she whispered excitedly, keeping her words private. She eased down onto the floor, her back against the plank siding. Her long arms were wrapped around her knees and she was staring into the dark corners of the candle-lit room. "The Underground Railroad," she explained, as if unable to believe her own words. "They will keep us here," she gestured at the interior of the small cell-like enclosure with a weary wave of her hand, "until it's safe to take us farther on."

"Farther?" Runaway sat up, his eyes on the woman's face. They were in the north. *Indiana*, he remembered, a free state. *Freedom is here*, he thought. He shook his head, rubbing at the tired ache in the back of his neck. *If not here, then where!? How much further do we need to go?*

"Canada," Charlotte answered as if she could read his mind. She turned, facing Runaway, her chin resting on her knees. "War," she said. "Between the North and the South, they've been at war since spring." She closed her eyes, her shoulder drooping, silent as she worked the thing over in her mind, sorted her thoughts. Discarding some, filing others away; finally speaking the rest. "Fugitive slaves are to be returned to their owners," she said. "It's the law." She stared at the bulwark of baled hay that hid them from the rest of the world. "The country-side is full of bounty men, paddy rollers.

"We've got to go farther north, someplace far away, away from the war, from Kentucky." Her words were so soft the boy could barely hear them.

"Can we trust these people?" Pictures – wide-awake nightmares — were beginning to form in the dark corners of Runaway's mind. Pictures of them being held in this place, cajoled unto thinking themselves safe as they were being fed and kept warm. *Fatted hogs*, he thought; *livestock being made ready for market, for slaughter*. He struggled to control his frustration. "Can we trust them?" he demanded, repeating his question, his fingers wrapped tightly around the woman's forearm.

"We have to trust them," the woman answered quickly. *Too quickly*. She unwound Runaway's fingers from her arm, grimacing in pain. "We just have to careful," she warned. She reached out, her hand on Runaway's knee. "One of us will have to watch at night; *every night*." She nodded at the others; the women who were already lulled to sleep by the quiet comfort of their full bellies. "*We'll* have to watch."

Runaway inhaled. He nodded his head and stood up, his bones cracking as he stretched. "I'll watch first," he said softly. "And then, tomorrow, during the day…"

The woman nodded. There would be many long nights and long days before it was over, before they were far away from this place.

Runaway stood up, stretching to ward off the tiredness and the feeling of fullness. *Freedom*. It was as far away as it had ever been, just as elusive, as intangible as in the beginning. Runaway propped himself against the uncomfortable roughness of the unfinished wall, a piece of straw in his mouth. Maybe they would never find it.

Maybe, for them, it had never existed.

***

Their progress was slow. Summer had turned to fall and already frost had begun to paint its lacy patterns on the drying cornstalks bound like Indian tipis in the dormant fields. Runaway and the women had continued their night-time existence, learning to sleep during the day as if they were night-prowling rodents, fully awake at moon-rise in the hope that this would be the night they could again continue their long journey.

They were in Illinois now. They had crossed the Wabash River by ferry just north of Vincennes and were heading for another station, Lawrenceville, on the northeast bank of the Embarrass River.

An old Conestoga wagon picked them up when the ferry docked, rolling out of the pre-dawn fog by some secret prearrangement with the Illinois abolitionists. It was a mystery to Runaway and the others, the efficient way the Northerners operated their secret organization. They called it the Underground Railroad, too. Complete with timetables, conductors; stations. The fugitives were referred to as freight or parcels. On occasion — when they were far enough north — they were called passengers.

Runaway and the others were still freight. The population of southern Illinois — like southern Indiana — was for the most part, Kentucky farmers who had migrated into the new Northwest Territories to settle the Ohio and Wabash valleys. Their hearts and loyalties still lay in the South and they were adamantly pro-slavery. They were also violently anti-abolitionist. The War had only intensified those bitter feelings.

The boy sat huddled in the back of the old wagon, his shoulders pressed into the corner. He was humming and Charlotte was beside him, quietly singing along. *One more river; there's one more river to cross...* The woman laughed, realizing the irony in the words, tiny lines at the corners of her eyes softening her face, her hand on Runaway's shoulder.

He understood her laughter, the gentle teasing sounds in her voice, and felt his cheeks color. The song had just come to him, from some forgotten corner of his mind, and he had hummed the melody without realizing the significance of the unsung words. *One more river*, he mused, smiling. It seemed that their long journey — their progress on their long journey — was measured by the waterways they had crossed. Even the conductors along the line marked their way by the rivers.

The wagon stopped, and the passengers were immediately quiet; apprehensive. Runaway strained to hear, holding his breath, listening to the hushed conversation beyond the heavy tarp. The voices were indistinguishable above the pounding of his heart, the noise of his own pulse. The early morning sun beat down on the heavy canvas, intensifying the heat in the interior of the dark wagon and the rising temperature made him sweat. The youth felt the perspiration beading at his ears, felt it well from beneath his skin, trickle across his forehead, and form in heavy droplets at his brows. The drops seemed to grow, hanging suspended above his eyelids until the sheer weight pulled them away from his face. They dropped in slow motion, cold against his clenched hands, with the measured regularity of a clock's ticking. But slowly, so slowly, as if time were dragging its feet.

Then — finally — the driver clucked to the team, slapping the reins across the broad backs of the two horses that pulled the heavy wagon. He drove on in silence for a long time, and then pulled into a shady spot well off the road.

The women welcomed the pause, scrambling down from the rear of the wagon, rubbing their eyes as they greeted the bright light of the sun. They were chattering, chirping like the busy, brown prairie hens, staying together as they headed into the brush to heed the call of nature.

Runaway kept his eyes on the white man who had been driving the prairie schooner. He was busy with a large tree branch, brushing the tracks of their wagon at the place where they had left the road. A white boy joined him, using a handful of smaller branches to rake the imprints of the heavy wheels from the long grass.

The young farmer straightened, his fist kneading at the tired ache in the small of his back, uneasiness in him as he surveyed the surrounding countryside. Silent, he pointed a long finger at the cloud of dissipating dust on the south-eastern horizon. "'Catcher's," he breathed, nodding toward the road. "They sent word from Lawrenceville that the fields are crawling with 'catchers." He was quiet again, turning to finger the harness leather.

Runaway reached out to the other. "How close?" he asked quietly.

The young man shrugged. "Too close," he answered. He stared at the boy for a time, his eyes shifting suddenly to the women. "We're going to have to try and get you across the river today, into Bridgeport." He shook his head. "Damned Copperheads," he swore. He reached out, his hand on the boy's arm, paternal, consoling. "They ain't caught us yet, boy," he said softly. "And they won't." He gave the boy's forearm a reassuring squeeze. "Get the others," he ordered. "We've got to go on."

Runaway did as he was told, the old resentments swelling within him when the white man ordered him into the woods to flush out the others. And then his anger mellowed. This was different than it had been on the plantations; the old man had spoken to him without any rancor, any harshness.

They crossed the Embarrass, using a narrow plank bridge that barely cleared the water, the hoofbeats of the shod team echoing hollow above the river. The boards rose and fell, clattering as the iron-rimmed wheels rolled forward, the slapping of the planks against the groaning crossbeams adding to the tenseness of the passengers. Then they were off the bridge, the horses moving out smartly as the driver used his whip to urge them on.

Runaway peered out from beneath the canvas top, his eyes on the acres of harvested fields that spread out on either side of the road. Large drying barns — the rust-red paint fading — dotted the countryside, the narrow slats revealing the amber and gold of hanging tobacco. In the distance, husked field corn radiated a bright yellow glow from the full corn cribs, fattening cattle and pigs rooting for forage in the harvested fields.

There was a feeling of tranquility to this place that gave a false sense of security for the young man and his companions. For months, they had remained in hiding, confining their movements to the nocturnal world of the owls. The world had changed around them without their being allowed to see, one season rolling quietly into another while they slept away the long days in hiding.

Occasionally, Runaway had observed uniformed soldiers, men passing unaware of his presence. They would pause on the farms where Runaway and the others were hidden, taking water, stopping for overnight bivouac before continuing on to the nearest rail head. The boy envied them. They were, at least, free to come and go during the day.

Buildings began appearing on the horizon with increasing regularity and the boy hunkered down into the darkness of the wagon again. Instinctively, as they always did when they approached a house or a village, all of them became quiet. He felt Charlotte's hand on his shoulder and reached out, his fingers entwining with hers.

"Soon," she whispered, her free hand on the growing bulk at her belly. "Soon it will all be behind us." She said the words as if saying them would make it so.

Chapter 4

Their stop in Bridgeport was brief. They were hurried into an old meeting house on the outskirts of town. They slipped inside the building, surprised by the flurry of activity going on inside the dimly lit rooms.

Plainly garbed women busied themselves around a long table. They had prepared a hot meal, steam rising from the heavy cast iron Dutch kettles and loaves of freshly baked bread. Other women were laying out fresh clothes, moving among the women as they held up cotton dresses and measured for fit.

The men were in the far corner at a smaller table, conferring in hushed vices as they consulted a large map. Runaway took his filled plate and inched closer to them, watching and listening as they spoke.

These men had a strange way of speaking, their conversation filled with biblical sounding *thees* and *thous*. There were six of them, an even half-dozen. Five of the men wore the same dark homespun clothing favored by the women, their faces prematurely aged by the carefully trimmed severity of their dark beards.

The other man — the sixth man — was clean shaven, his speech and manner as different as his appearance. He was a big man, tall, with fair hair and blue eyes, and there was something cat-like in the way he moved. There was no question in Runaway's mind that this man was the leader of this group. The others listened to him, stroking their beards, silently nodding their heads in approval. "Vandalia," he said finally. "I can take them as far as Vandalia." He tapped the map with his finger, the single digit drumming solidly on the table.

Their eyes met then, Runaway and the stranger's. The tall man's brow furrowed, then smoothed, and he nodded a silent greeting. He then swung his gaze to the woman, his eyes narrowing as he spied Charlotte. "She could pass," he said quietly, addressing the other men. "She could pass for white."

As one, the other five turned, facing the place where Charlotte stood. They nodded their heads in agreement, their hats bobbing up and down in unison.

****

Runaway stood outside the narrow door at the rear of the hall. He had been given new clothes; a pair of tan-colored pants and a neatly mended white shirt. His toes felt cramped in the high leather boots and he grimaced in anticipation of pain as he tried a few short steps across the broad plank flooring. Surprisingly, the boots were not as confining as they first felt and he was secretly pleased. In all his life, he had never worn or owned a pair of shoes, any shoes.

The door at his back opened and he turned, his mouth dropping open. Charlotte stood in the doorway, framed by the light from the single window at her back.

She was beautiful! The dress she wore was a simple frock, dark green with tiny, multi-colored flowers that seemed to grow in wild profusion all over the dark background fabric. A green sunbonnet covered her near-auburn hair. For the first time, Runaway saw that she had green eyes; green eyes with little flecks of brown. She stepped across the threshold, her laughter sounding like tapped crystal. Smiling, she took Runaway's hands. She was wearing gloves, white gloves. "Well?" she asked.

Runaway shook his head. He dropped her hand, clicking his heels as he backed up a step and bowed. "Ma'am," he drawled, trying hard to suppress his smile.

The big man joined them, intruding on their shared joy. He nodded his approval. "A fitting dress for the wife of a prosperous farmer," he smiled. He offered the woman his arm.

Charlotte cocked her head, her eyes losing some of their humor, becoming cold, suspicious. She reached out and then withdrew, her hand hovering between them for a brief moment. And then she curtsied and took the man's arm, returning his smile.

***

They traveled overland by open wagon. Charlotte rode on the seat beside the man, an openness and gaiety in her that Runaway had never seen.

The others — Runaway and the three women who had made the long journey with them — sat in the back of the wagon. The women's resentment of Charlotte had worsened since her transformation. They would exchange looks with one another and then stare hard at her back, mimicking her every move with great exaggeration, whispering among themselves. *Uppity nigger*, they snorted, contemptuous. Not only were they jealous of her better clothing, they were jealous of her place beside the man. *Of her light skin.*

Runaway tried hard to ignore their grumblings. From the beginning, he and Charlotte had been separated from the others, by differences not of their own choosing, differences that had set them apart.

Their ability to read, their genteel way of speaking that had come with the long years of in-house servitude. Runaway drew his aching legs up to his chest, resting his chin on his knees. *I don't care*, he thought bitterly. *I don't give a tinker's damn what they think.*

It wasn't true. He did care. The lack of acceptance by the whites was something he expected, it had been a daily, life-long occurrence. He had only to look at the whites to know that he was different. But to be rejected by his own people, by people of his own color, just because he could read, or because he spoke differently... He shook his head, not understanding. It seemed that he and Charlotte hovered somewhere between two diverse worlds, one black, one white, unwanted and not fitting into either one.

The boy reconsidered. He didn't seem to fit. But Charlotte... Runaway's jaws tightened and he felt an anger building deep in his chest. Charlotte seemed to be thriving in her role as a white woman, seemed content, pretending to be something she was not.

They made camp at dusk, pulling well off the road into an unharvested orchard. The fallen apples popped beneath the heavy wagon wheels, spicing the air with the acrid odor of pungent juice. The women clambered from the wagon, seeking out bits of fruit to munch on, polishing the red and gold skins against their skirts as the two men laid the fire for their evening meal.

Runaway sulked through supper, his still full plate on the ground at his right knee. Even the aroma of the fried apples Charlotte had prepared failed to appease his growing bad temper. He refused to talk to the woman, leaving her questions unanswered. In the end, she quit trying and withdrew, going back to the fire.

Back to her white companion. Runaway watched as they worked together to finish cleaning up the dishes from supper, angry at the snatches of laughter that drifted to him on the evening breeze.

It was growing cold, the temperature dropping with the sun, a damp chill rolling into the orchard in thick white clouds that hugged the cooling earth. The white man was on his feet, tending the dray stock, securing the ropes that held them tied to the picket line. Man and animals seemed to hover legless above the ground, their bodies severed by the cold mist, yet somehow able to move.

Finally, the man finished his chores. He glided across the clearing, cutting through the haze with long, purposeful strides. "Warmer by the fire, boy," he said. He reached down, patting Runaway's shoulder as he passed.

Runaway stiffened at the man's touch. He bolted upright, his fists knotted at his sides. "I have a name," he breathed, the words coming through clenched teeth.

The big man stopped, half-turning to face the youth. "So do I," he said quietly, measuring the boy with his eyes. "Cooper," he volunteered, extending his right hand. "Jonathan Cooper."

The boy's brow knotted and he stared down at the man's pale hand. The hesitancy was two-fold. Mistrust, first, the same suspicions that had always haunted the boy as well as resentment, bitter resentment at the way the man had caused a breach between him and Charlotte. Runaway unclenched his hands, rubbing the palms against his thighs, his eyes still on Cooper's outstretched hand. "Runaway," he said, at last, a pride — an arrogance — in the single word, in his tone. He lifted his head, facing the man, choosing to ignore the proffered hand.

Cooper returned the boy's scrutiny, withdrawing his hand. "It's still warmer by the fire," he said quietly, nodding toward the women.

Runaway followed the man's gaze, his eyes dwelling on the others. The three field women were huddled together, laughing, playing jackstones in the dirt. Charlotte was on a pallet near the fire, apart from them, purposely excluded by the others. Alone. *For now*, the boy though bitterly, thinking of the way that Charlotte and Cooper would spend their time later. Talking, always talking. *Sharing*. "No," he said, shaking his head at Cooper's invitation. He clenched his fists again, pressing his arms against his sides to stop the chill that was creeping through his body.

Cooper stood his ground, digging into his pocket for his pipe and tobacco. He took his time with the pipe scraping out the bowl with his long thumbnail. "Did it ever occur to you that this is the safest way?" he asked, his voice soft. He tamped the tobacco into the pipe, taking great pains, his movements slow, deliberate. "You have no papers, none of you and the law — if you're caught —" he was sucking on the pipe, his hand cupped over the flickering matchstick, "...war or no war... will hold you as fugitive slaves." The pipe was going nicely now and Cooper paused to savor the sedative bite of the nicotine against his tongue. "Charlotte is..."

"... Playing at being a lady! A *white* lady!!" Runaway interrupted, his words louder than he intended.

Cooper reached out, clamping a massive hand on Runaway's shoulder. "*Is* a lady," he corrected. He carried the rebuke one step further. "A *grown* lady," he continued, sweeping the boy's face with his eyes. There was no pretense in the man or in his verbal chastisement. He could not afford risking the safety of himself or the others because of a love-struck boy whose continued spells of jealousy jeopardized their charade. There were already too many problems, too many dangers. Cooper released his hold on the boy's shoulder. "She's with child," Cooper observed, the red glow from his pipe bright crimson against the moonless sky. "She'll need a man to take care of her…"

The rage that had been gnawing at Runaway's belly bit at him with a force that brought pain, real pain. Without thinking, he swung at Cooper's head. "She's mine! I'll take care of her!!"

Cooper blocked the blow, his hand closing around the boy's forearm. "No," he said, the words soft, whisper quiet on the night air. "She belongs to herself now, not you." He held on to the boy, cutting him with his words. "When the time comes, she'll choose her own man. *Man*," he said, repeating the word, his voice louder.

They stood there, locked together, the man's hand still around the boy's arm. Runaway shook his head, not wanting to believe the man's words. Charlotte was special, from the beginning, she was special. The difference in their ages didn't matter.

Had never mattered. She needed him. And he needed her. "She's mine," he said again. He had loved her, had made love to her. It had been his first time and it was good and it was forever. He pulled away from Cooper, swallowing at the dull ache in his throat. "*I'll* take care of her," he said stubbornly. He faced Cooper again. "Me.

I'll take care of her."

Cooper's brow knotted, and he searched the boy's face. *My God*, he thought. *He thinks I want her! He thinks that we've...* He shook his head. "We'll have to watch tonight," he said aloud, exhaling a thin stream of blue smoke, the pipe stem clenched between his teeth. "While the women sleep, we'll have to watch." A puff of smoke trailed the final word.

The boy cocked his head, the anger still clawing at his belly. "Watch?"

Cooper nodded, the dying red embers from his pipe marking the up and down movement of his head. "You've a long way to go, Runaway, before you find freedom." He was quiet a moment, remembering how he had said these same words to the Octoroon. "Vandalia, north to Springfield and then on to Chicago." He recited the itinerary as though he had made the trip many times. Runaway followed after the man as he headed back to the wagon, listening to him, their disagreement forgotten. "Across Lake Michigan," Cooper continued. He drew the route in the air with a wave of his hand, the pipe water-falling a tiny shower of crimson ash, "up to the peninsula." He paused, reaching into the wagon, beneath the seat. When he withdrew his arm, he was holding a Spencer carbine. "Canada," he finished, loading the piece. "Toronto, maybe or Montreal."

"How far?" Runaway breathed. "How long?"

Cooper closed the breech on the Spencer, muffling the click with his palm. "A thousand miles," he answered. "Maybe more." *There is no kindness in a lie*, Cooper thought, *and sometimes even less kindness in the truth*.

Runaway slumped against the side of the wagon. A thousand miles. "How long?" he asked again.

Cooper canted the carbine on his right shoulder. "Six months," he answered. "If we run into problems, a year." *Before the War — before Secession — it would have been half that,* he thought, remembering. He continued. "Never, if we don't watch our backs."

Runaway turned, burying his head in his arms. He began to weep, great sobs coming from the depths of his worn body, his tired soul.

Cooper went back to the fire. He bent down on one knee, talking to the woman, his mouth close to her ear. Charlotte listened for a time and then shook her head, her hand on her the growing mound at her belly. There was nothing she could do for the boy. Not now. *Not ever.*

***

Elisha Montgomery stood beside his horse, his eyes on the plank bridge spanning the Embarrass. He cursed, softly at first, and then out loud. "Goddammit, Caleb! Use the whip!!" He began pacing, watching as his younger brother poked and prodded at the bay mare that pulled the small buggy. She balked, mouthing the bit, her ears working as the youth tried to force her onto the bridge a second time. Montgomery cursed again, a long string of swear words exploding into the morning quiet. He led his gelding to the rear-end of the buggy and tied it off.

The narrow bridge was wide enough for only one vehicle to cross at a time and Caleb had pointed the mare's nose right down the middle. As it was now, there was barely enough room for Montgomery to edge beside the wagon. He turned sideways, sucking in his belly as he headed toward the mare's head.

There was a breeze, a soft breeze, rattling through the

leaves that hung brown and dry from the tall trees that bordered the river. The noise added to the mare's nervousness and she rolled her eyes, trying to watch all things at once, kicking out at the man as he came up beside her. "Bitch!" Montgomery lifted his left hand, knotting it into a fist. He punched out at the mare's head, striking her hard between the eyes. Then he grabbed the cheek strap on her bridle, twisting the leather until the bit cut into the sides of her mouth. Keeping a tight hold, he pulled her forward, jerking hard on the leather when she bolted at the sound of her shod hooves against the loose planks.

He led her across the bridge, pausing on occasion to swear at his brother. "The whip, Goddammit! Use the whip!!" he roared.

They completed the crossing, the mare's mouth and neck flecked with bright red blood and white foam. Montgomery turned loose of the horse's bridle, his gaze on the horizon. He was getting closer. He could feel it, smell it. Closer to the woman and the boy. He reached up with his left hand, kneading the useless stump at his right shoulder. *He was going to find them, all of them. And when he did...*

***

Cooper left them at Vandalia, slipping out of their lives as quietly and as mysteriously as he had come. Runaway missed the man. They had been together ten days, moving leisurely across the Illinois prairie, across still more rivers and streams. The Little Wabash first and then the Kaskaskia, to yet another barn and another hiding place. And then they would wait, for another underground conductor to take them farther up the line.

They were waiting now for Charlotte's child. Her labor had begun early in the morning before the sun had risen. They were hiding in an abandoned farmhouse, a two-storied frame building with soot-blackened ceilings and littered floors. But it was warm, warm and tight against the cold fall winds that came more and more in the grey hours just before dawn.

The women were with Charlotte. They had shooed Runaway from the room, working hard to make the woman comfortable. Their petty quarrels seemed forgotten as they took turns sitting with her, trying hard to ease her pains.

And then, just before the first light of morning, Runaway heard the faint sound of something — something very small, very weak — gasping for air. There was a feeble cough — silence — and then another whisper-soft wheeze and then the sharp sound of flesh striking flesh, followed by the angry hurt cry of an infant. The cries subsided gradually and were replaced by the soft *ooohs* and *aahs* of the women.

Runaway headed toward the sounds, feeling the intruder. Things had changed between him and Charlotte. They had fought, after that first night with Cooper and they had not spoken since. Still, he wanted to see the child. And the woman.

He was surprised when she beckoned for him to come in. The women backed away from the straw bed, opening a path for him. "Charlotte," he greeted. The others left then, as if by some prearranged, secret agreement.

The small room seemed to grow in size as the others filed out. Runaway stood just inside the narrow doorway, pensive, undecided. As if he could not decide if he really wanted to be here. And then Charlotte turned to face him, and he felt a pleasant pain deep in his chest, the same sensation that had always been there when he looked into her face.

She waved him closer, the baby an indistinguishable bundle of make-shift swaddling clothes. The child was making tiny, feeble sounds. A small fist appeared, the tiny arm stretching, the minute, fragile fingers wound tightly around an unbelievably small thumb.

The arm was white.

"It's a girl," Charlotte breathed. She was propped up against a mound of blanket-covered straw, her face radiant, her cheeks flushed; bathed with her own sweat. "Come see, Runaway." She held up the child.

Runaway was remembering the pale arm. He half turned, staring at the door, the darkness of the room beyond it, his body tensed as if he were going to run. Then he closed his eyes, his shoulders drooping. Reluctantly, he turned back to the place where the woman laid, his step slow, heavy, as he crossed the room.

Charlotte pulled the bit of colored flannel away from the child's face, the tiny head. Runaway inhaled sharply, not meaning to, and — feeling guilty — reached out. He extended his forefinger, tickling the baby's pink palm. The infant opened the tight first and then closed the tiny fingers around the boy's single digit. The contrast between the colors of their skin was even more pronounced. "Elisha," he whispered. "She belongs to Elisha." There was an agony in his words, a bitter anguish. He had actually hoped that another man — another slave — had fathered the child.

Charlotte stiffened, pulling the child away. "Yes," she said, the strain in her voice, the anger. "Elisha is her father." She swung her head around, facing the boy, her right eyebrow arched in a sudden defiant hostility. "She's mine, boy. *Mine!*" She clutched the child to her breast, a fierceness in her.

There was a long, tense silence between the boy and the woman, the room quiet except for the sound of their breathing. The woman was cuddling the child close to her breasts. Gently, she took the baby's hand in her own, her fingers stroking the soft velvet of the baby's cheek, lingering — smoothing — the straight softness of the child's pale hair. "She will be able to pass, Runaway. Look at her," she held the child up again. "She'll be able to pass."

It was true. Runaway felt his heart tumble to the bottom of his stomach. The child's features were a subtle blending of Charlotte's and Elisha's. *Even the eyes*, he marveled. The child's eyes were going to be light, lighter even than Charlotte's. Runaway felt sick inside, sick and angry. He had lost Charlotte to this child, to the light skin the mother and child shared. Desperately, he reached out, his hand closing around Charlotte's. "I love you," he breathed. "I want…"

The woman shook her head. She was staring at Runaway's brown hand, the difference between her own skin and his. "I'm not going north anymore, Runaway." She pulled away from him, staring straight ahead, her voice soft, firm. "I'm going as far as Springfield and then…" She was somewhere else now, transported away from this place by her dreams. "…and then," she continued, "I'm going to find work." There was a single tear rolling down her right cheek. "For her," she said softly. "I'll lie, cheat, whatever I have to do." She bit her bottom lip, fighting back the tears, gently rocking the baby back and forth. "She's going to be free, Runaway. Really free.

"She'll be white. People will look at her and know she is my daughter, and they will think that I am white as well."

Runaway stood up, brushing off his pants, picking at the non-existent bits of straw long after the real ones were all gone. He couldn't look at the woman anymore, the woman or the child.

He'd lost her. Whatever there had been between them whatever they had shared, none of it mattered. It was as if they had never been together as if all the pain was for nothing.

Chapter 5

———

There were two conductors this time. Younger than any of the others, garbed in the simple homespun of the men Runaway had seen before, the men who spoke as if they were reading from the Bible.

It surprised them that these men were armed. Not as Cooper had been. These men carried weapons more suitable for hunting game than for defense. They carried their shot and powder in oilcloth packets in their jacket pockets, like farm boys out hunting pheasant.

They were Quakers. Runaway found out soon after they began their journey. Young men opposed to the Government's plan of conscription, the drafting of young men to fight a war in which they did not — because of their pacifist beliefs — support.

They could have bought their way out, could have paid someone else to serve in their place. But they considered this wrong, too, to ask someone else to bear arms in their place, against their brothers.

Runaway did not understand their thinking, the way they referred to all men as their 'brothers'. White and black alike, they felt that all men were their brethren; that God — their God, at least — considered every man equal in His sight.

There was another thing about these gentle souls that Runaway did not understand, their dedication to the ideal that no man could legally or morally hold another man in bondage. He wondered if any Quakers lived in the South.

The journey progressed slowly. The young men were fearless in their chosen task, fearless but inexperienced. Twice, they misjudged their calculations, missing an appointed meeting with the conductor that would lead them further north. They consulted for a time, trying hard to conceal their confusion from the others, and then decided to go on.

The delay and their miscalculations caused other problems as well. They were traveling on short rations now, scavenging for food from the land much as Runaway and the others had when they first began their long trek. During the day, they hid out in the cornfields, or in the high prairie grasses of untilled and unclaimed land. They moved on again at night, fighting both time and the weather.

Under the cover of evening, they forded Macoupin Creek, the water seeming to penetrate their skin and chill the bones. Two of the women were sick, their movement sluggish; wet, terrible coughs taking hold of them and punishing their tortured lungs. The men ministered to them as best they could, but it was not enough.

They camped, late one night, southwest of the small settlement of Virden. One of the Quakers went into the town, returning with a supply of dried meat and herb tea. For the first time in more days than Runaway could remember, they risked a fire.

***

Elisha felt a strange elation. He had contacted a man in Vandalia, an old friend of his uncle's, a man whose loyalties lay with the Secessionists. The man was a merchant, a buyer and seller of things. *Of information.* For two bottles of Kentucky bourbon, the old man told him everything he knew about the Abolitionists, about their network of underground stations. People were eager to talk. The war was going badly for the North, and the farmers in southern Illinois were quick to align themselves with the outnumbered but victorious Confederate army.

Elisha used their doubts. He traveled north, buying more information with the Yankee gold he carried in his money belt.

He was just south of Virden when the strange euphoria gripped him. It was the same feeling he had experienced whenever he neared his quarry, whenever he knew that the game he was tracking was within his reach.

Caleb was still with him, driving the small covered buggy. They had traveled all day and well into the night. And then they saw the smoke.

***

Runaway and the others lounged around the small campfire, moving their simple pallets close to the circle of light and warmth. Their bellies were full, and the strong, hot herbal tea had lulled them into a sense of safety and well-being. They were warm, warm and content.

The younger of the two Quakers was the first to fall. He had been at the fire, pouring himself another cup of tea. There was nothing to warn them, no sudden rush of feet, no calling out, just the single loud shot.

Runaway was on the opposite side of the fire. He looked up and saw the face of the young white man before him. The man opened his mouth as if to speak, his eyebrows rising in a look of surprise, surprise and sudden pain. And then, without a sound, he pitched forward, falling across the fire.

They froze, all of them. And then the women began to scream. Runaway grabbed the one nearest him, his eyes searching the clearing for Charlotte. She was gone, a brief flash of flowered cloth marking her departure, and then she disappeared into the high grass. Instinctively, Runaway followed, dragging the other woman with him. Beside him, the other Quaker sprinted to keep up, while at their backs they could hear the terrified wail of the other two women they had left behind.

Runaway caught up with Charlotte, reaching out his hand to restrain her. "Get down!" he ordered. He shoved her roughly to the ground, pulling the other woman down beside them. The remaining white man did not fare so well. He stood up, fumbling with his rifle. And then he was on the ground, in front of Runaway, his dead eyes staring up at the boy.

Runaway grabbed for the rifle, taking the gun from the dead man's hands. He dug into the man's pockets for the remaining powder and shot. And then, without looking back, he began to snake-crawl away.

Charlotte and the other woman followed after him, running in a half crouch, their labored breathing cutting into the black silence that surrounded them. It was harder for Charlotte. She was carrying her child, the baby pressed against her breast as she struggled to keep up. They were climbing now, moving up the face of a small hill. Winded, they paused, their backs pressed into the damp earthen bank of a dry creek bed.

They could see the campsite below them. Runaway heard Charlotte inhale sharply and turned to follow her gaze. She was staring directly at the still-burning campfire, holding her breath, watching as Elisha and Caleb came into the dim circle of light.

Elisha went to the fallen man, toeing the corpse and rolling it away from the fire. The front of the dead man's coat was smoldering, the putrid smell of burnt flesh blending with the noxious odor of charred cloth.

It was then that he called out to Caleb. He set the younger man to work on the two women that cowered beside their pallets, watching as his brother began pummeling them with the butt of his rifle, beating them about the face and shoulders. They screamed, loud, their tormented cries fading to noiseless, open-mouthed whimpers.

Caleb shackled the women, putting the heavy leg irons in place around their ankles. The arm bracelets were next. He clamped them in place, one on the right wrist, dropping the other end between their feet; pulling the wrist chains under the leg chains; then up. He yanked hard, until the women were forced to bend at the waist, and then shackled the other wrist.

There was no way the women could run. They were chained in a bent-over position and totally helpless. Caleb was beside them, doing his crazed jig, prodding the women with a stick.

Elisha was busy elsewhere. He picked up the stack of wood from beside the fire, throwing the dry branches onto the glowing embers. The dry limbs crackled and popped, finally catching, the yellow flames whooshing high above the circle of rock. Then he turned, facing the place where the runaways hid. "Charlotte!!" He roared the woman's name above the sound of the fire. "I want you, woman! Now!!"

Charlotte sucked in a great breath of air, her hand going to her mouth. Elisha loomed before the fire, a brooding, angry god, his left hand raised to the heavens. The cool night air stirred, lifting the folded sleeve that hung limp and empty at his right side.

Montgomery called the woman's name a second time, screamed it. Like some fallen angel taking roll call at the gates of Hell. *"Charlotte!!"* The single word exploded into the night, echoing again and again. "I'll find you, woman. You and that nigger cub! *I'll find you!!"*

Its sleep disturbed, the baby began to cry; a soft, uncomfortable whimper at first, and then the high-pitched wail of hunger. The cry tore into the darkness, rousing the night birds and prompting them to answer.

Elisha's face changed. The anger was replaced by a look of wild elation, of victorious discovery. He bent down, scooping his rifle up from beside the fire. Waving his brother away, he sprinted into the darkness, following the sound.

Runaway pulled at Charlotte's sleeve. The other woman was beside them, and they began to move again, cursing the darkness and the unknown terrain. The baby's cries were more intense, the infant nuzzling at Charlotte's breast and finding only the coarse fabric that covered her mother's nipples. Runaway was pulling Charlotte along beside him. "You've got to keep her quiet, Charlotte..."

The woman pressed the baby to her bosom, stifling the cries. They ran on, the three of them, Runaway in the lead, carrying the rifle that had belonged to the dead Quaker. The terrain was inconstant, clumps of buffalo grass topping clusters of dark peat. The up and down rise made their legs ache, their chests heaving with the uneven effort of their crippling run. The other woman fell, collapsing in a heap, her head buried in her arms; her shoulders shaking in quiet sobs of defeat.

They broke out of the bog into a flat field, their hearts pumping as they continued to run. They could hear Elisha behind them; heard his exultant whoop as he found the fallen woman. There was another sound, the dull thunk of Elisha's rifle butt against the woman's head; a measured blow to put her out. And then they heard the steady thump of his boots as he began his pursuit anew, moving quickly through the grass, gaining.

The small clearing gave way to a broad expanse of orchard, lower limbs of the dwarfed trees tearing at their clothing as they ran. Runaway was still in the lead, moving easily now, shifting the heavy rifle from his right to his left hand.

He stopped running, catching Charlotte and pointing silently to the dark entrance of a small thicket. Shoving the woman ahead of him, Runaway forced her into the narrow opening, scrambling in after her.

They rested, biting their lips to suppress the noise of their labored breathing. The thicket and the surrounding orchard became eerily silent. There was no sound from Elisha; just the noise of the night wind in the dry leaves that still hung from the lower branches of the dormant trees.

Charlotte was strangely quiet. She began rocking back and forth, slowly at first, and then more rapidly. She pulled the child away from her breasts, studied her for a time, and then pulled her close, the rocking more hurried.

Then she stopped and was completely quiet. "She's not crying," she said suddenly, her voice barely audible. "She won't cry anymore," she breathed, something childlike in her tone, the words coming in an odd singsong. She held out the child for Runaway's inspection.

The baby was dead. The tiny body lay limp and warm in Charlotte's outstretched arms. Something compelled the boy to look closer. The baby's mouth was open, the skin around its nose and mouth a strange blue white, a small amount of white froth at the corner of its mouth. The tiny eyes were open, sightless. Runaway pulled away, sick at heart in what he was seeing.

The child had suffocated.

Charlotte laid the baby on the ground. She was crooning; softly, more to herself than the dead child. Carefully, she arranged the baby's blanket, her movements gentle. She was whispering to the child, her words hurried, desperate. "It's going to be all right," she said. "We'll be free soon. We'll be free and living in a fine house." She touched the child's feet. "You'll have fine, white shoes and a new dress for every day."

Horrified, Runaway watched and listened; listened to promises that Charlotte was making, promises she could never keep.

Finished, Charlotte tucked the soft blanket around the child's body. She lifted the baby to her shoulder, patting her back. "We have to go now, Runaway," she said, nodding at the baby; "To Springfield." She reached out, her hand warm on Runaway's cheek. "You come and see us sometime, Runaway." She caressed the boy's cheek, her fingers lingering when she felt the warmth of his tears on the back of her hand. Puzzled, she withdrew her hand. "In the spring," she said. "You come see us in the spring." And then, she reached down, taking the rifle that lay at the boy's knee.

She was gone, the baby still against her shoulder, the rifle in her free hand. She moved quickly into the orchard, her step sure. Runaway started after her and then stopped. The narrow crescent of a new moon peeked out from behind the cover of a bank of grey clouds, lighting the orchard and illuminating the woman's face. The boy watched, transfixed. There was madness in the woman's face, a wild insanity. And then the woman's features softened, and she clutched the baby to her shoulder, a strange tranquility touching her mouth and eyes as she looked back to the place where Runaway stood. She mouthed the words "good-bye", and then moved off again.

Runaway ducked back into the thicket. He heard the loud metal click as Charlotte cocked the rifle, watching as she headed back toward the campsite. "Elisha! *E-e-li-sha!!*" She kept walking, shouting the man's name again and again.

"I hear you, woman!" Montgomery answered her calls. He stepped out of the trees, his legs spread, waiting.

Charlotte hefted the rifle, resting the butt against her hip. "No more, Elisha!" she shouted. She pulled the trigger, a flash of light preceding the explosion.

Montgomery stood his ground, the shot clipping his left ear. With slow deliberation, he lifted his own weapon, took aim, and fired.

Charlotte screamed. She pitched forward onto her knees, the baby falling to the ground. "Run!" She screamed. She was fumbling to reload the rifle. "*Run!!*"

Realizing now what the woman intended, Runaway broke from his hiding place, his head pounding. He raced into the darkness beyond the orchard, his arms pumping as he fled. He could hear the woman still screaming at him, hear her as she begged him to flee. And then there was another shot, just one, then silence; total, complete silence.

***

The woman stared into the darkness of the loft, her eyes adjusting to the darkness. She was not old, and certainly not young, yet there was something about her that gave the impression she could take care of herself no matter the situation.

Runaway returned her stare, shrinking back into the darkness. He had no choice but to stay where he was, nor any desire or strength to move. His whole body ached and there was an emptiness inside him that made him sick.

The woman spoke first as if understanding the things that had happened to the boy. "Thee needs more than a place to sleep, child. Thee needs a good cleaning and a hot meal." She kept her place on the ladder, her voice soft and gentle.

It seemed to Runaway that she was not aware of his color and he wondered to himself if she were blind. He shook his head at the foolishness of his thoughts, still not moving from the place where he crouched.

"Thee can speak, can't thee?" The woman's voice was caring, her words coming with a tenderness Runaway found difficult to comprehend. He had been alone so long, so damned long.

"I can speak," he said finally. He still had not stood up, afraid that his size would frighten the woman, sure in his fevered mind that she thought him a small child. He shrunk further back into the corner, trying to make himself smaller.

The woman moved up into the loft, careful not to force her presence on the boy while avoiding any sudden movements. The sun filtering through the roof touched her hair and made it shine like a new copper piece. She cleared her throat, looking off into the distance beyond the barn as if looking to the land for her words. "My son used to do that. When he was not yet a man, but grown beyond his boyish things. It was as if he wanted to make himself smaller, so that I could hold him close to me again, like I did when he was just a baby." She was quiet again, fingering the hay. She looked across at Runaway, her smile sad. "He wasn't much older than you when he left here. Sixteen," she said, judging the boy's age by his size, her voice fading into a quiet, pensive silence.

"I reckon I'm about that old, Ma'am." Runaway moved from the corner and stood up, stretching to ease the soreness in his legs.

"Thee doesn't know thy own age?" The woman didn't wait for an answer. "Of course thee doesn't. Thee would be fortunate to know thy name."

"There are those who call me 'boy'." Runaway said the word arrogantly, his tone filled with a bitter sarcasm.

"Then they are fools," the woman returned, her eyes dancing as she measured the youth with a long, sweeping gaze. "From thy size, they would do well to call thee 'Man'."

Runaway followed the woman's eyes to his worn jeans. Weeks ago — so many weeks ago — they had hung on him. They had drug the ground and covered his toes and he had held them in place with a belt woven from grass.

He couldn't remember when had thrown away the belt, or when he had lost the button that fastened the pants at his waist. He had noticed only the passing of the days, the hours of daylight and darkness he had spent hiding and walking.

The woman reached out to him, her hand resting gently on his arm. "I have shamed thee, child. Can you forgive me?"

He looked into her face, searching beyond her pale eyes. Never before in his life had he been asked to forgive a white person anything, and the idea of the woman asking — begging — filled him with a feeling he had never experienced. "No," he said, his voice almost a whisper. He waited, expecting the woman to strike out at him. When she didn't, he repeated the word, louder, shaking his head. "No!"

The woman patted his arm softly, nodding up at him. "Thee come to the house when thee is ready. Thee needs a good meal if thee is to continue thy journey."

Runaway watched as the woman turned back to the ladder, sorry that he had spoken harshly, yet unable to undo his words. He moved to her side, steadying the ladder as she turned and climbed down, watching the sun in her hair.

She brushed the hay from her dress when she reached the barn floor, shading her eyes as she looked up into the loft. "I thank thee," she called, waving up at him.

He watched as she left the barn, following her with his eyes as she crossed the well-tended yard to the house. She paused at the arbor gate, reaching down to cup the single yellow tea rose in her hand, lingering there for a time as she mourned the last rose clinging to the near dormant vines.

Runaway gazed down at his mud-caked feet. He had discarded the boots a long time ago, the soles worn completely through. There was a thick coating of dirt on his pants as well, and he brushed at his knees, slapping his hand against the cloth and marveling at the perfect imprint of his hand the remained. "Damn!" he breathed. He had been too busy running to care about how he looked. He decided that the woman would have to accept him as he was and started down the ladder.

He spied the pump as he crossed the yard and the towel and basin that sat on the bench beside it. The items hadn't been there when he had first looked down from the haymow and he wondered how he had missed seeing the woman place them there.

Runaway had forgotten how good water without the stench of the river could feel against his skin. There was no green slime to cling to his hide, no smell to sicken him and stick to his body. He enjoyed the cleanness of the toweling and the sweet scent of the bar of soap that kept slipping through his fingers.

"You would do well to use the trough, boy."

Runaway dropped the soap, the sound of the man's voice filling him with the old fear. His legs refused to work and he found himself unable to turn around, his eyes pasted to the bar of soap that lay on the ground at his feet.

A man's hand closed around the soap, a massive hand, well-tanned and full of strength. It was the last thing Runaway saw. His knees buckled beneath him, his heart beating as though it would burst from his body, and the earth moved up to meet him.

The big hand dropped the soap back into the dirt and reached up to catch the boy as he fell. "Rebecca!" The man lifted the boy into his arms, calling for his wife. Without waiting, he carried the boy up the steps and across the porch.

The woman was waiting, holding the door open as her husband hurried into the kitchen. She pointed into the darkness of the small bedroom off the kitchen, following behind the man. Quickly, she moved ahead of him, fluffing the pillows, reaching out to help ease the boy onto the narrow bed. "He's burning with fever, Jonathan." Her hand moved to the boy's forehead.

Jonathan Cooper's hand tensed against the woman's

shoulder. His brow furrowed, and he reached out to the youth, cupping his hand as he turned the boy's face into the light. "Runaway," he breathed. He shook his head, not believing. "We'll need the doctor, Rebecca." He began loosening the boy's collar. "He's sick, very sick."

Rebecca Cooper canted her head, studying her husband's face. "Does thee know him, Jonathan?" she asked quietly.

Cooper nodded his head, his hand pressed against the boy's neck, his fingers searching out a pulse. "I know him," he said. He stared across at his wife. "He's a fugitive, Rebecca. He was with the others I picked up at Lawrenceville, the ones I took to Vandalia."

The woman inhaled, her eyes returning to the boy. "Thee knows the danger of keeping him here, Jonathan," she said quietly.

Cooper pulled a blanket from the trunk at the end of the bed and covered the shaking youth. "I've known other danger, Rebecca. Of my own making..." He reached out, taking the woman's hands. He was in agony, thinking of the peril he had inadvertently brought to their doorstep. He still didn't understand how Runaway had found him. "I'll move him as soon as I can, Rebecca."

"Thee will not," she answered firmly. "Thee will go for the doctor." She touched the man's cheek with her hand. "It is time that I shared in your work, Jonathan. Past time." She smiled and kissed him. "The doctor..."

Cooper pulled the woman close in a quick hug and then he was gone.

Chapter 6

Rebecca busied herself in the kitchen. She had sent the girls to their room, telling them that they must stay there until their father returned. They went without arguing, somehow sensing the boy's illness, tiptoeing across the floor and down the hall.

The woman went to the sink, pumping water into a basin. She welcomed the sound of the pump, the way the squeaking covered the frightened, delirious cries of the boy. He was calling out now, shouting names, a single name, she realized, Charlotte, over and over again, the same name. Then he was quiet.

Rebecca returned to the bed, bathing the boy's forehead with the cool water. She shuddered at his renewed cries, somehow knowing that he was calling out for someone who would never answer. Then he reached out to her, grabbing her hand like a baby trying to walk, but afraid to fall.

The sun was disappearing behind the hills, dropping below the row of trees at the edge of the road, the shadows reaching out at the house like long fingers and the woman felt a degree of concern she had never experienced before.

She was anxious for her husband and worried even more about the girls. She knew only too well the danger in hiding fugitive slaves — her father's barn had been burned because he had sheltered a small group of refugees from South Carolina — and that danger had increased ten-fold since the War had begun.

The sound of horses on the road roused the woman from her dark musings, and she held her breath, counting the cadence of plodding hooves. There were two horses, one being ridden and the other pulling a wagon. A frown touched the corner of her mouth. If it was Jonathan and the doctor, it would have been the lighter sound of a buggy. Assuming they were going to pass by, she turned back to the boy, bathing his face and chest, feeling the heat of his skin increase beneath her fingers. He was shaking now, his teeth chattering. The woman left him for a moment, going to the chest on the far wall for another blanket. He fought her as she tucked it around his shoulders, the woman holding fast until the struggling ceased.

It was then that she heard the sound of the fence gate opening; the fence leading from the road. There was a slight pause, and then the noise of a single horse, heavy, moving at a slow walk. Following the big horse, she heard the quick, mincing trot of a second, smaller animal, along with the rattling noise of a small wagon. She listened as both animals approached the house and finally stopped.

The woman hurried to the kitchen, pausing at the window. She did not recognize the two men or their animals. Quickly, she turned back to the doorway of the small bedroom, closing the door. Her gaze darted about the room, looking for anything that would indicate anything was amiss; then, satisfied that nothing appeared out of the ordinary, she returned to the window.

She studied the two men from behind a small separation in the gingham curtains. There were two men, one mounted on a large blood bay, the other driving the small wagon. There were women with them, three Negroes; small, pitiful creatures huddled in an unnatural posture in the back of the wagon. Rebecca considered her options, and then breathed a short, simple prayer. "Thy will, Father." Her calm restored, she went to the kitchen door, opened it, and stepped out onto the porch. "Gentlemen?"

Both men removed their hats, startled by the directness of her greeting. The eldest one spoke, his teeth yellow with tobacco stain. "Water, ma'am," he said, turning to point at the trough; "and maybe something to eat?"

Rebecca pulled the door shut behind her, her hand still on the knob. Her voice was soft, but there was a steely resolve in her words. "Thee are welcome," she said softly, "but" she nodded in their direction, focusing on the tell-tale bulge beneath their long coats, "not thy weapons."

The men exchanged glances. They could smell the salty, rich aroma of freshly baked bread. The mounted man spoke, his voice as soft as the woman's. "These are hard times, ma'am," he said, smiling, "and the work we do requires these weapons."

Rebecca canted her head, one eyebrow arching as she struggled to hold her temper and her tongue. She gestured toward the women in the back of the wagon. "Thee has already done thy work," she ventured. She lifted her head. "Thee may eat; thee, and the women, but thy weapons will remain outside."

The older man dismounted. He stood beside the horse, tired, his head pressed against the saddle, his left hand knotted in a tight fist on the pommel. He sighed, a loud, clearly audible sound that seemed to come from the depths of his belly. Silently, he stood there for a time. And then he knotted the gelding's reins around the fence post.

He came up the stairs, his younger brother jumping from the wagon seat to follow after him, impatient, the smells from the kitchen enticing him, increasing his hunger. Rebecca — her hand still on the doorknob — watched the pair as they came up the stairs, their boots thumping loudly against the hollow blackness below the stoop. For the first time, the woman realized that the older man had only a small portion of his right arm. She was filled with pity for him, the compassion swiftly fading as he neared her. He stood towering above her, so close she could feel the warmth of his breath against her forehead. He spoke, his hand closing around hers as he forced the door open and shoved her into the room. "We'll eat, woman," he said, his face hard. He jerked his head toward the buggy. "The others can go to hell." He paused, waiting for the woman to move, angry when she still refused to step aside. "Ma'am," he breathed, "I've been chasing niggers for the last three weeks. I'm tired, tired and hungry. And I'm feeling mean, real mean." He released his hold on the woman, brushing aside his coat so that his pistol showed.

Rebecca pulled herself erect, rubbing at her wrist. "Thy mother would be ashamed of thee. This is a home, not a battlefield, and not a place where one man delights in the pain of another." She stood aside, contemptuous. "If thee are still afraid, then so be it. I'll not harm thee," she declared, raking the men with her eyes, "and neither will my children." She turned her back on the men, feeling their eyes on her as moved across the room to the stove.

The men moved to the table, each choosing a chair that allowed them to face the open door. Their eyes moved about the room, searching out the corners, looking for some sign that the woman was deceiving them; that there was something that she was hiding. A door opened at the end of the hall and Montgomery half rose from his chair, his hand on his pistol.

Rebecca behaved as though nothing was out of the ordinary, ignoring the man's sudden movement. She spied her daughter, Elizabeth, peeking from behind the door at the end of the hallway. Shaking her finger at the child, she chided her, her voice calm and soft. "Thee are to stay in thy room, Beth, thee and thy sister," she scolded. The child's head disappeared, the door clicking loudly as she eased it shut.

Montgomery's hand was still hovering above his pistol. "Your man," he demanded. "Where is your man?"

Rebecca returned to the stove and began preparing the plates of food. "We have a large farm," she answered. "He's tending to the stock." She was already silently praying that God would forgive her for the lie.

"And there's no one else?" Montgomery had been on the hunt for a long time; maybe too long.

Rebecca faced the man, seeing the mistrust. She returned his gaze, staring into his eyes. "Only my children," she said firmly. She placed the full plates before the men and went back to her chores.

The men ate greedily, calling for more food and coffee. Still, they were unable to relax, always listening, watching. Even when Rebecca took food to the women in the wagon, the men did not trust her out their sight, as if in fear that she would summon some secret army to devour them. It was an irrational fear but they could not dismiss it.

Rebecca returned to the house and was immediately aware of the continued tension. Her own concerns had increased, her mind reeling at the possibilities that lay before her. There were so many *what ifs*. What if the boy regained consciousness and stumbled out of the bedroom? What if Jonathan returned home while the men were still there? What if…

There was a sudden sound from the front bedroom, from the darkness beyond the closed door. The boy called out, loudly, in a voice that was definitely masculine, and not that of a child. Rebecca stood rooted in place, her hand trembling as she poured Montgomery what she had hoped would be his final cup of coffee. She placed the pot on the table, backing up as Caleb leapt to his feet, his pistol in his right hand as he struck out at the woman, catching her on her lower jaw. "She lied, Elijah! The bitch lied!!"

Rebecca tasted blood in her mouth and her fingers moved to her tingling lips. She was now between the men and the darkened bedroom. Montgomery moved to push her aside, cocking his pistol as the voice behind the door screamed out yet again. The woman grabbed at the man's arm. "No!!" she shouted, struggling to keep him from finding the secret hidden behind the closed door. She stood her ground, her eyes sweeping the man's face. "It's my son," she lied. Still, she could not stop the tears, the memory of her own boy still fresh. "He has typhus," she whispered. "*My boy is dying from typhus.*"

Montgomery paled, stumbling over his own feet and his brother's as they both backed up toward the front door. The pistol hung heavy and useless in Elisha's left hand, useless against this unseen enemy. The screams from beyond the closed door had diminished to be replaced by a loud, wet hacking punctuated by an ominous wheezing.

It was enough to convince both men that the woman was being truthful. Elisha shoved his pistol into his belt and then wiped the back of his hand across his mouth. "Caleb," he called. He reached out, knocking an unfinished biscuit from his brother's hand. Together, they bolted for the door, Caleb knocking over his chair in his rush to leave the house.

Rebecca could hear them as they ran across the porch, relieved when both horses left at a full run, the small wagon tilting precariously on two wheels as they turned and raced out of the driveway. She collapsed against the door jamb, watching the dissipating cloud of dust that marked their departure. She began to weep then, burying her head in her arms. She hadn't really lied. It was true what she had said about her boy. He had died of typhus.

Soldiers had brought him home, the same soldiers who had lured him away from the farm with their talk of a Holy War, of the *Great Cause.* What they hadn't told her son — what, in their youth, they probably hadn't known themselves — was that there was no such thing as a Holy War. All there was were young boys who perished in a political chess game instigated by old men seeking to feed their own greed, to fill their own selfish needs.

They had stacked the dead at Manassas like cordwood, she had read. All those fine young men and for what?

The boy cried out again, rousing Rebecca from her bitter reverie. This is what her son thought he was dying for, what Jonathan continued to risk his life for, this poor, sick child who did not know his age or have a proper name. A boy who lived with fear as his constant companion, without a decent home, without even the simplest comforts, a boy who preferred death in some swamp to the nameless horror of bondage.

Rebecca returned to the boy, reaching out to wipe away the sweat at his forehead. *No man had the right to do this to another,* she thought. *No man had the right to take from anyone what God had so freely given.*

***

Runaway's recovery was slow. The years of deprivation on the plantations and his recent trek north had robbed his body of the natural recuperative powers of the young. Rebecca and Jonathan tended him, day and night, willing him to live. In the first weeks of his illness, it had seemed a losing battle.

Fall passed, yielding to winter, the muted brown of the sleeping countryside soon covered with the total whiteness of the season's first snow. Runaway sat propped up in the same bed where he had lain so long, his fingers scratching — tracing — the delicate patterns of the frost that rimmed the inside of the window. He had never seen snow and watched in awed silence as the two little girls, Elizabeth and Naomi, frolicked on the white landscape.

They were dressed in heavy, bulky woolen coats. Black, like the knit stockings and cotton dresses they wore. Rebecca had tied long scarves around their blond heads, wrapping them around their necks until only their ruddy cheeks and wind-burned noses shone.

Elizabeth was busy building a snowman, patting the small mound into the shape of a ball. She dropped the clump into the ankle-deep snow at her feet, kicking it before her with one booted foot until it began to grow. Then she bent forward, a considerable task because of the awkward bulkiness of her clothing, and began pushing the thing with both hands. She stopped, pausing to wave at Runaway, lifting a mittened hand in a brief salute. Then she was gone again, pushing the growing ball before her, making a zigzag path through the damp snow, Naomi following behind her. Bit by bit, their lop-sided snowman began to take shape, the largest ball at the bottom, a smaller one in the middle. They placed the smallest one on top and then disappeared into the root cellar to search for a carrot nose. And then they were done. And just as quickly the snowman was forgotten.

They played a new game now, cutting a circular track in the snow, their voices rising and falling with the wind. Runaway could hear them. He watched, wishing he could be with them, and then reconsidering. He lay back against the pillow, watching as Elizabeth perched on her heels, arms outstretched. She fell over on her back, sweeping her arms up and down at her sides while moving her legs in scissors-like precision, flattening the snow. When she stood up, her imprint remained. It was, Runaway realized, an angel. *A snow angel.*

The little girl waved at him again and then turned to chase her sister into the barn.

Runaway envied them their freedom. He was still imprisoned, by his illness this time but most of all by the color of his skin. He wondered if he would ever have a life beyond this room, beyond this house.

There was a gentle knock at the door and Cooper entered, a covered tray balanced on his arm. Tea, of course, the boy knew. Rebecca had great faith in the healing powers of her herbal tea.

"You're getting restless." Cooper sat down on the chair next to the bed, shoving a mug into the boy's hand.

Runaway nodded. "It's been a long time," he said, sipping the hot liquid. He stared out the window again. The girls were nowhere to be seen, the landscape barren without them.

Cooper nodded his head. He reached inside his coat pocket, taking out a packet of papers. "It's going to be longer," he said. He smoothed out the top sheet of paper, his finger tapping against the printed page. "The War is still going badly for the North," he said. "They're calling for more volunteers…"

Runaway studied the man's face. He knew from the time he had spent in their house that while Rebecca was a Quaker, Jonathan was not. He supported her in her beliefs, even attended services with her, but there was something about the man … "Will you go?" he asked finally.

Cooper took his time before answering, his brow knotted. "No." He raised his eyes, meeting the boy's gaze and seeing the unasked question. For some reason, he felt a need to answer what hadn't been asked. "I promised Rebecca." He was quiet again. "We lost our son to the War," he said softly. He was staring out the window now, his blue eyes fierce, angry. "He was raised in the Faith and he still chose to go." As always, he found himself wondering if — had he been at the farm — he could have stopped the boy, could have kept him at home. "Rebecca…" he had trouble finding the words. "Rebecca took it hard.

"The Society is important to her. She defied it once when she married me. And then…" He shrugged, unable to continue. The Society had strong stands against the War, any war. For a man to voluntarily join the army — to serve — meant expulsion. That had hurt Rebecca the most, that their son had died outside the fellowship. Cooper shook his head, his hand rubbing at the dull ache at the base of his skull. He loved Rebecca passionately and without question. But he had never understood her beliefs. He faced the boy, eager to change the subject. "The railroad isn't carrying freight anymore, Runaway. The War…" Everything seemed to revolve around the damned war.

The boy absorbed the words, his face showing no emotion. "I'll be well enough to travel soon," he said finally.

"If there's no one to take me then I'll go myself."

Cooper stood up, his hands shoved into his pockets. He had expected as much. "It will be too dangerous now." He began pacing, up and down, his feet thumping across the braided rug. "You'll have to have papers; papers saying that you are free. Or…" he faced the boy then, his hands still behind his back; "…or you can stay here." The next was more difficult. "You can stay here, as a slave."

Runaway's head snapped up and he bolted upright in the bed, his eyes wide. Cooper waved the boy's attempted argument aside, his manner brusque. "We've done it before," he said. "When there have been unexpected delays; when someone has gotten sick." He wasn't speaking of himself and Rebecca — he had always kept her aloof from his work with the Underground, fearing for her safety. "We use forged papers, forged bills of sale. Then we pretend," he stressed the words, "…*we pretend* the man or woman belongs here. After a time, we give them their papers — their freedom — and they can move on.

"In the daylight, in the *full* daylight, traveling like any free man."

Stubbornly, Runaway shook his head. Even pretense was too much. The idea of pretending to be anything less than free sickened him. Besides, it could be a trick, just another white man's trick. He immediately felt guilty at the thought, but he still could not yield. "No," he said softly.

Cooper's face colored and he stood at the end of the bed, his fingers wrapped around the brass railing. "There's no other way," he said firmly. He raised his hand when the boy tried to interrupt. "That first day, when we brought you into the house. Two men came, two catchers." He stopped letting the words sink in, remembering the long talks he and the boy had had when the fever finally broke and released its hold on the youth's mind. "A big man," he said, his eyes on the boy. "A big man with one arm…"

Runaway sank back into the down pillow. "Montgomery," he said. Just saying the name brought it all back, the things that had happened in the cornfield, the things that had happened when Montgomery found them. *Charlotte, and Charlotte's child.* He stared up at Cooper. "Why didn't you tell me? Before?" He felt the sting of tears welling at the corner of his eyes.

"You weren't well enough," Cooper answered. "The time wasn't right."

"How long?" The boy asked the question, and then laughed, remembering he had asked the man the same thing once before, a long time ago. "How long will I have to wait?"

Cooper shook his head. "I don't know," he said quietly. He had never lied to the boy, and he wasn't going to start now. "I just don't know." He decided it was time to tell the rest. "It's not just you I'm concerned about, Runaway," he continued. "This is a family, my family. Rebecca and the children, they come first, before you, before me.

"They will always come first."

Chapter 7

They continued their charade, greeting the New Year with guarded joy and bittersweet celebration. January 1862 ushered in a renewed hope for the North but little hope for Runaway.

Part of their pretense meant exposing Runaway to their neighbors, making him seem a natural, unassuming part of the small community. He worked beside Cooper doing the many tedious chores required on the small farm, learning to hate the bone-eating snow that had at first entranced him but was now just one more aggravation. There never seemed to be enough warmth, no matter how many socks he put on, or — late at night — beneath the thick down quilts that covered him.

The work was not hard, not in the sense the work on the plantations had been hard. And Cooper was an easy 'master'. He never asked any more of Runaway than he was willing to do himself. They shared the work, just as they shared the benefits of their labor.

Runaway had become a part of the family without even realizing it. He ate at the table with everyone else, leaving the room only on the rare occasion when someone other than a Friend or a neighbor happened to call.

Or when his manners failed him or he yielded to his temper when Elizabeth would plague him, or he teased Naomi and made her cry. Cooper would raise his hand, one finger pointing toward the hallway, or Rebecca would raise an eyebrow and Runaway and the girls would know they had gone too far. They would ask to be excused then, knowing that it was expected, and would beat a hasty retreat to the refuge of the front room and the warmth of the brick fireplace.

Cooper took it on himself to improve the boy's education. He brought piles of books down from the trunks in the attic, waving aside Rebecca's objections as he filled the boy's head with the pagan stories from Greek mythology. Winged horses, and men who attempted to fly, Runaway read them all. Avariciously, with a hunger that was kindled by each new story.

They taught him the practical things, too, at Rebecca's insistence. She labored at the table with all three children, teaching them the elaborate, flowing script she had learned as a girl. She taught him grammar and math, too, for the time ahead when he would seek a job and make his own way. *If Farmer Jones had two pecks of apple, and he sold half* ...

Spring came, with the rush of wind and rain, the snow disappearing as it had come, the earth brown and alive again. It was raining the afternoon Runaway went into the attic, seeking out more books to read. Elizabeth and Naomi followed after him, chattering the way eight-year-olds tend to prattle. Runaway often tired of the girls' constant questions but he never tired of their company. Not that he would tell them that for they would just become more bothersome. But they were his family now, and sometimes ...

...sometimes, he even forgot he was different.

"Look!" Elizabeth tugged at Runaway's sleeve. She and Naomi had found an old mirror frame. The glass was gone, the oval frame suspended by a pivot screw midway on a claw-footed stand. It was tall, taller than the two girls. Elizabeth stood on one side, Naomi on the other. They were dressed in identical dresses, their long hair in pigtails. They stood facing each other, mimicking each other's movements.

It was like looking in a mirror, Runaway thought, watching them. He had never seen twins before knowing Elizabeth and Naomi, not that he could remember and he paused in his search for a book to watch them. Naomi reached up with her right hand and Elizabeth did the same with her left, pressing her palm against her sister's palm. They stood there, making great circles with their hands touching, both of them trying to keep a straight face. Elizabeth began to move her arm faster and faster.

Elizabeth tended to be a troublemaker. As identical as the two girls were in appearance, they were different in temperament. It was as if Naomi had inherited the subdued, quiet nature of her mother, while Elizabeth...

Elizabeth had the robust, sometimes volatile spirit of her father, and the same sense of adventure. And every so often it came to the surface. Runaway knew from watching her eyes that it wouldn't be long before she did something to purposely provoke — no, challenge — her sister.

Finally, she did. She kept on with her flurry of movements until Naomi got angry and made a face. Elizabeth quickly stepped through the frame and punched her sister right in the nose.

Even Runaway was surprised. "*Elizabeth!*" he whispered the girl's name, mindful that the door leading to the downstairs hallway was full open. He grabbed the child, tucking her under his arm as he pulled her away from Naomi. He deposited her on the floor, turning to tend to the other child's bloody nose.

Elizabeth paid no mind to her sister's noisy sobs. She had found something new to interest her. Far back under the eaves, tucked in a corner she had never explored.

It was a seaman's chest, ornate, with brass fittings and thick leather straps. She began digging at the buckles, pulling the leather through until only the center strap remained. That one was larger than the others and the hasp more difficult to manipulate. Finally, she pulled the strap free. The trunk lid lifted easier than she had anticipated, thumping against the wooden crossbeams where the roof sloped downwards.

Runaway was at her shoulder. The chest was crammed full. There was blue wool jacket with tarnished brass buttons and matching trousers. Beneath the clothing, an officer's cap; white dress gloves, and a sword in an ivory and gold-trimmed scabbard, and next to the naval armament...

A ship's log.

Together, Runaway and Elizabeth opened the leather-bound book, exposing the faded pages. There, in the heavy stroke both of them knew so well were the words:

The Ivory Queen

J. T. Cooper, Ship's Master

Runaway leafed through the book, hurriedly at first, more slowly as he began to piece the words that were at first a pale brown, and then — farther along — a bold, glaring black against yellowing page.

A slave ship! Cooper had been master of a slave ship!! Runaway choked back the tears that burned in his throat, oblivious to the things around him, his head swimming. He couldn't believe what he was reading; didn't want to believe. And yet, there it was, in Cooper's own hand.

The journal recorded his voyage. *Voyages,* Runaway realized. Neat, precise lines of words recording places, times. *3rd April. Took on board this day one hundred twelve niggers…* Runaway inhaled sharply at the word. In all his time with the man, he had never heard Cooper use the hated epithet. He shook the contradiction away, compelled to read on, *… one hundred twelve niggers; forty male; sixty-seven young females fit for breeding; five infants.* Runaway continued to turn the pages; slowly, one by one, his chest tightening as the rage clutched at his very heart. *18th June. Sighted two naval frigates first watch flying U.S. colors. Am being pursued.* He turned the page. *19th June. Third frigate sighted northeast; one shot fired across bow at first light.* There were no entries for the next three days; and then one whole page that was blank. Then, at the top of the next, one short entry, as legible and as straightly aligned as the others. *24th June. Two frigates still in pursuit. Disposed cargo overboard, third watch…*

Runaway had been on his knees in front of the trunk. He shifted position, sitting down hard on the floor, the book resting in his lap. He thumbed through the pages a final time, still refusing to believe. The words seemed to leap out at him, the entries made regarding the human cargo Cooper's ship had carried below its decks. Notations the man had made during the two-and-a-half-month voyage from the coast of Africa to the Gulf of Mexico, concluding with the final entry: *Disposed cargo overboard, third watch.*

There had been only one kind of cargo on board the Ivory Queen. Niggers. One hundred twelve niggers.

"Elizabeth?" Cooper's head appeared above the

rimmed opening that led to the rooms below the attic. He came up the last few steps slowly, his eyes adjusting to the dim light.

Runaway watched the man, his hand tightening on the edge of the leather-bound log. They exchanged a long, silent glance, their eyes meeting, Cooper's lips a tight line as he saw the pilfered chest. The man didn't raise his voice, didn't say anything to the youth. He stepped up into the attic, his gaze shifting to his daughter. "You've been quarreling with Naomi again," he said softly. He pressed his finger to the girl's lips when she started to protest and used his free hand to swat her three times on her small rear end. "Go downstairs, Elizabeth," he ordered softly. Sniffling, the child obeyed.

The silence hung between them, between the boy and the man, the soft sound of the rain that pattered against the shingled roof growing louder. Everything in the room seemed to sharpen, intensify. The odor of cedar chips and camphor packed away with the stored clothing; the steady *drip-drip-drip* of the small leak at the base of the red brick chimney.

Runaway held up the book, his hands shaking. "Is it true?" he whispered. It was worse than if he had shouted. *"Is it true?!"*

"It's true," Cooper answered. Just the two words; no explanation, no excuses. *No remorse.*

Runaway stood up, his chest heaving. He was torn by a whirlwind of feelings, his stomach churning. He had slept and eaten in this man's house, accepted his friendship. And now this. He felt a great sense of betrayal. He lifted the book, shoving it at the man, the journal a growing barrier between them, a wall of living ice. "How did you do it, Cooper!?" His voice came in a cold, hushed whisper.

"How do you *dispose* of one — hundred — twelve — *niggers*!?" The number, the exact number, seemed important.

Cooper's voice matched the boy's, his blue eyes the color of ice. "You throw them over the side," he answered harshly. He ducked when the youth threw the book at him, moving his upper torso only, his feet firmly planted on the floor. Reaching out, he grabbed the boy's arms, one hand on each shoulder. He held the boy tight until the struggling stopped. "You throw them in the water," he said again, his eyes on the far wall, the window. The grey rain was like the sea the way he remembered the sea on that last voyage. "You stand on the deck and you watch them sink. You hear them cry out — hear the sound of them as they fight against the chains —" The man paused, clearing his throat as if he were going to speak again. He did not. Instead, he released his hold on the boy's arms, lifting his hands away and backing up.

The anger Runaway had felt earlier had not diminished. He struck out at Cooper again, his arms flailing, cutting through the damp air. He could hear the sound as his fists struck the man's chest and shoulders. Cooper stood there, his hands pressed against his sides, taking the blows in utter silence. Winded, Runaway stopped. He leaned back against the warm chimney, his shoulders rising and falling with each labored breath. Cooper had never moved. The boy stared at him, clenching and unclenching his fists, wishing himself stronger. "You hypocrite!" he roared, not caring who heard him. "You goddamned hypocrite!!

"I hate you. God, how I hate you!!"

Cooper smiled, a sad smile filled with a melancholy that had haunted him for more years than he cared to remember. "I can understand that, boy," he said softly. Instinctively, as he had done before many times in the past few months, he reached out, his right hand hovering at the youth's shoulder. He withdrew it when he saw the boy flinch and draw away. "I hated, too. For a long time," he said softly, taking a deep breath. He dropped his head, his eyes narrowing, hands stuffed deep in his pockets. "I was twenty the year I took the Queen as my own," he began. "I'd been on board her since I was fourteen, just fourteen.

"That was the year my father died," he said, his tone changing, a hardness in his features and his words. "1839." He was quiet again, reflective, struggling with memories had buried along with his own tortured past. "My father was a ship's master," he continued, "an owner. He was shipwrecked off Cuba, waiting for a way to work his passage home.

"There was a Spanish schooner, the *Amistad*. The owners needed an experienced officer to serve as second in command, someone familiar with the waters. My father needed a ship.

"He had never transported slaves before," Cooper continued, clearing his throat. "Not once." He shook his head, still — after all these years — not understanding the thing. "They were well out to sea when a slave named Cinque led the others in a revolt.

"They murdered my father." The edge had returned to the man's voice, to his face. "Hacked him and the Captain to death with cane knives, and threw what was left of their bodies over the side." Cooper turned, facing the boy, something dark and sinister deep in his eyes. "That's when I learned to hate. Then, and two years later when the courts released the Africans and sent them home.

"That was when my mother died." Cooper was at the trunk now. He reached down, fingering the brass buttons on the decaying jacket. "I wanted revenge," he breathed,

"For all of it. My father; my mother; my younger sister and two brothers who were taken away to live with strangers …" the old feelings were creeping back, tearing at the man in the same way time had ravaged the fragile fabric beneath his fingers. Years later, when he had tried to reunite with his siblings, his sister was dead from scarlet fever and his brothers … He had never found his brothers. Suddenly, he flung the coat aside, slamming the trunk shut, his face white. "I loved my parents, Runaway. I loved my family. And I lost them all because of…"

Runaway faced him, "… some niggers who wanted to be free?!" He was shaking his head, unable to balance what he had heard with his own perception of what had occurred. "They killed your father and the captain." He held up two fingers. "Two men. And you slaughtered a hundred and twelve." The enormity of the deed sickened the boy and he felt a wave of nausea sweep over him.

Cooper wouldn't — couldn't — let it go. "More," he said coldly. He was thinking of the slaves who died during transport, the ones too sick, too frail to survive the poor rations and the filthy quarters. "I sailed on the Queen for six years before she was my own." He grabbed the boy's arm, pulling him close. "Slaves, Runaway. That was the only cargo she ever carried." He held on to the boy. "It was a long time ago," he said. "I was a different man then.

"It was a different time."

Runaway pulled away again. "It doesn't make them any less dead, Cooper. Does it?" His eyes narrowed. "Does Rebecca know?" He didn't wait for an answer. *"Did your son know?!"* The sudden pain he saw in the other's face gave him a moment of smug satisfaction.

Cooper's face was flushed and the large vein at his temple was throbbing. "He knew," he answered, his voice a hoarse whisper, something more than sorrow in his words, *guilt, a father's guilt.* Cooper's entire body was shaking. "It's why he left to fight in Mr. Lincoln's war."

That Runaway had not expected.

***

The alienation between Cooper and the boy continued. They still worked together, laboring side by side in the fields and barn but rarely speaking. Rebecca watched them, wishing it was within her power to heal the breach and make it better. Her best course, she decided, was to leave it all in God's hands.

Unless, she had thought ruefully in a moment of weakness, *God was too busy.* That was when she had pulled the seaman's chest out of the attic and — with the girls struggling to help her — carried it out into the yard and set it afire. It had been a magnificent blaze, one that had prompted Elizabeth and Naomi to dance around the flames like the ancient Illinois Pottawatomie but even that had not helped purge the dark pall that hung over the homestead.

Spring and summer passed silently away, fading into a glorious fall. The harvest had been like the brilliant colors that adorned the fields and the orchards, abundant. The meat had been smoked and cured, the last of the vegetables canned and the potatoes and cabbages stored away in the stone cellar beneath the summer kitchen. The land was falling asleep again, snug beneath the layer of fallen leaves and the cow droppings Cooper and Runaway had diligently spread to nourish the dormant fields. It was a never-ending cycle, planting, tending, harvesting and then renewal. It was as if the earth mirrored life.

Cooper rose with the sun, saddling the grey mare, leading her away from the house before mounting. He was proud of the animal, the one vanity he allowed himself, and pleased with the way she responded beneath his fingers. A thoroughbred, she was born to run, and she did, a joy in both man and animal as they pounded across the fields. Cooper kept her under a tight rein, the balls of his feet nesting firmly in the stirrup irons. He leaned forward, his weight over her shoulders, urging her toward the stone fence that bordered the field on the southwest corner of the farm. The mare took the jump without breaking stride, all four feet clearing the wall cleanly.

She would bring a good price. *More than enough*, he thought.

He would miss her, but it would be a proper penance, to give up something he loved to make things right for the boy.

*** *

It was late when Cooper returned to the farm. He walked back from the village, a five-mile trek that allowed him time to think. Absently, he balanced the parcel he was carrying, mentally going over the items that were secured inside. The list had been months in the making, ever since that night in the attic when he and Runaway had faced their shared demons.

He picked up the pace, feeling the wind against his face, and knowing from the smells that Rebecca had outdone herself preparing supper. The aroma of roast chicken and cornbread stuffing beckoned him, along with the rich bouquet of strong coffee. Cooper was surprised at that, for coffee was a rare thing now.

The girls were setting the table when he came up the

pathway and Runaway was helping them, the sound of the laughter soft, good natured. Cooper climbed the porch stairs, his steps purposely heavy. Elizabeth heard him first. "Papa!" She was through the door and in his arms, covering his neck with warm kisses.

"Smells like Christmas," Cooper said, smiling across at his wife. He nodded at the unspoken question in her eyes, removing his coat. "A fit meal for a celebration," he declared, turning back to the table.

They took their places, Rebecca quieting the girls before saying Grace, her hand on her husband's arm. Then, without any further ceremony, they feasted. They topped off the meal with a still-warm shoo-fly pie and when they were through, Cooper picked up the package that had lain at his elbow.

"For you," he said simply, shoving the packet in front of the boy. Runaway hesitated. Cooper pushed the package closer, releasing it. "Your papers," he said. "Three copies, all signed and witnessed, along with two letters verifying your good character."

The boy picked up the parcel, staring at it. He tore at the light twine, working it loose, and then — in frustration — finally broke it. The wrapping unfolded, the contents spilling out onto the table. It was like Cooper said. Runaway fingered the documents. There was also a small stack of currency. They were all silent, watching him.

"Thee are free, Runaway," Rebecca said softly. "Thee are truly free."

Chapter 8

Cooper was in the barn when Runaway found him, bedding down the livestock. The boy picked up a pitchfork, lifting a forkful of hay over the side of the milk cow's pen. "Rebecca said you sold the grey mare," he grunted, shoving the fork into the pile of cut timothy. "To pay for my papers and to give me the money I'll need to travel."

Cooper wiped his brow. He was leaning heavily on his own fork. "You earned it," he said. "It's been more than a year, Runaway. You've done your fair share and you've done it well." The man meant every word he said.

Runaway looked around the barn. Something wasn't right, something more than the mare's being gone. His eyes swept the corners, resting finally on the chestnut gelding that stood tethered and saddled by the open back door. He swung his gaze back to Cooper, studying him. And then he knew. Cooper was dressed as he had been that first time when they had first met. *When Cooper came to lead them to Vandalia.* "I don't need you this time," the boy said, bristling.

"Not everything is about you, Runaway," Cooper said

quietly. He crossed to where the gelding stood, lifting the stirrups to check the girth straps. "The Railroad is transporting freight again," he announced.

Runaway joined the man, suddenly interested. "But the War...?"

Cooper faced the youth. He dug into his pocket and pulled out a torn piece of newspaper. "Lincoln issued a proclamation," he said. "They're calling it a *Preliminary Emancipation Proclamation.*" He didn't wait for the boy to read it. "It says that as of January 1st, all slaves in all states — even those in rebellion — will be free. *Forever free.*" The man was checking his bedroll now and the cavy kit he carried behind the saddle. "The slaves in the border states," he paused, strapping on a cartridge belt that seemed to appear from nowhere, "some of them are making the break now." Satisfied, he pulled the belt tight, fastening the buckle.

The anger that had consumed Runaway during that long-ago evening in the damp attic swelled within him again. "Why?" he asked. "Why do you go after them?" He crumpled up the piece of newspaper Cooper had given him, heaving it into a corner. "Is it to salve your conscience or to try and buy back your soul?!"

Cooper continued with his preparations. He was checking his pistol now. "To make amends," he said quietly. He faced the boy. "To try and give to someone else the things I took away from all the others."

They stood there for a time, the breech between them as wide as ever. Cooper was the first to speak. "Three hundred thirteen," he said cryptically. "That's how many slaves I brought into Cuba, to Mexico and Texas, as master of my own ship." He raked the boy with his eyes. "I've brought almost that many up from the South." His voice lowered.

"Three hundred, counting you and the others I brought to Vandalia." This time when he looked at the boy, he was smiling. "Just thirteen more…"

Runaway snorted. "And then what? You'll have bought my forgiveness just like you bought my papers!?"

Cooper laughed, but there was no humor in the sound, only a bitter irony. "*Your* forgiveness!? I don't need your forgiveness, boy! Just God's; God's, and my own." He shook his head. "I don't owe you anything, Runaway. I never have. The people I owe are dead."

The boy stood there, thinking on the man's words, thinking of all the things he had learned in the man's house, with the man's family. He had seen so much love in that house, had felt so much love. But try as he could, he could not make the hate — the unforgiving hate — go away any more than he could take the man's hand. "I owe you a debt," he said quietly. "And I owe Rebecca." He knew how the woman felt about Cooper's work with the railroad. "I want to go with you."

The older man shook his head. "No." He reached out, his hand on the young man's shoulder. "You want to go for all the wrong reasons, Runaway." He was chastising the boy, refusing to hold back. "I told you before. It's not about you, what *you* owe, what you don't owe, what *you* feel." He paused, considering the words before he said them. "It's about the people, Runaway. *Your* people. And you don't give a damn about the people.

"In all the time you've been here, all you've been concerned with was your own freedom, no one else's. Just yours." The words continued to pour out, all the unsaid words he had held inside for so long. "You've been doing the same thing these past months you accused Charlotte of doing, pretending that you're something you're not, as if the world beyond this farm doesn't exist.

"You're no different than I was, boy. You hate what's convenient to hate when it's convenient. Charlotte's dead so you can't hate her. And Montgomery's not here. So that leaves me." He shook his head. "I never hurt you, Runaway. I hurt the others but I never hurt you." He whispered the final words, his hand still on the boy's shoulder. He let go, turning back to the gelding. "There'll be a wagon coming for you in the morning. One of the men from the Society will take you as far north as Springfield. You'll be able to take a train north from there, as far north as you want." He mounted the horse, moving out of the barn at a walk. "Luck, boy," he called over his shoulder. And then he disappeared into the darkness.

Runaway watched after the man, listening as the sound of the gelding's hooves were swallowed up by the same blackness that had devoured the man. And then it was silent and there was no more noise but the sound of his own breathing.

He trudged back toward the house, his thoughts filled with the same turmoil that tugged at his heart. It was true, all of it, everything that Cooper had said. In all the months that he had been in this house, he had never given any real thought to anyone other than himself. All his energies, his fear — even his hatreds — had been channeled into one narrow path, his desires, his dreams, and his freedom.

He had been wrong. He had stayed in this house without giving one thought to the risk that Cooper and his wife were taking. The even greater risk Cooper was taking right now.

Runaway opened the screen door and stepped into the kitchen, grateful that Rebecca had sent the twins to bed. She was at the stove, warming the last of the coffee. "I'm going after Jonathan," he said softly. "There are things I need to tell him."

Rebecca turned to face him. She had a large packet in her hand, a canvas sack similar to the cavy bag Cooper carried behind his saddle. "I've packed two clean shirts and an extra pair of pants. Thee will need your coat." She gestured toward the pile of things stacked on the chair next to the door and smiled.

He put on the jacket, marveling at the woman's wisdom and wondering if Cooper hadn't known as well. "I'm going to help him, Rebecca. I promise you, I'm going to help him bring those people out."

***

Runaway sat with his back against the rough wooden plank walls of the barn, his face towards the door. He hated keeping watch, straining his eyes and ears against the silent cold blackness that cloaked the world between midnight and the first grey light of dawn.

He rubbed his arms, surprised at the smooth tightness of his muscles. He had grown considerably since that long-ago day when he first started his run for freedom and he was still growing. *Almost six feet*, he mused. *Almost as tall as Jonathan.*

He rested his arms on his knees, propping his head in his cupped hands, staring into the darkness beyond the barn door. Sounds reached out to him, night sounds. He could hear the leaves moving across the packed earth of the stockyard, heard them whispering to him about the journeys. They had come into being with the spring, had grown old, and were now dying and had never moved from this place. He found himself envying the leaves.

Someone in the barn coughed and Runaway turned towards the sound. They slept so soundly, all the others who were with him. They trusted him to keep watch, all of them. From the ancient old man huddled against the far corner, to the young girl sleeping at his side, her hand clutching his shirttail, her thumb in her mouth.

The boy reached out to the girl, his hand pausing above her belly. He wanted to touch her, to feel the baby that was growing inside her. She was so young, much younger than he was, and she was going to have a child.

His hand dropped to the straw beside the girl and he eased down beside her, his head propped up on his flat palm. His mother must have been like this but he couldn't know that for sure. All he could remember about the woman that had borne him was that she had been so young, so very young. He was two, maybe three when he was taken from her and even though she was heavy with another child, he remembered his mother looking much as this girl looked now.

She never talked to anyone. She was just there, moving among them as quietly as a shadow. Runaway didn't even know her name or where she had come from or how she came to be with them. It almost seemed as though she had simply appeared among them, not there one moment, then walking beside him the next.

Restless, Runaway stood up, careful not to disturb the girl, gently unwinding her fingers from his shirt. He knew from the position of the moon that it was still early, that the night would be long for him. He moved towards the door, stepping over the still forms that covered the floor and then stood staring out into the darkness hoping that the cool night air would sharpen his senses.

"You'd think as we went on with this, it would become

easier." Cooper came up beside Runaway, his arm resting affectionately on the boy's shoulder. He was glad the boy had followed after him, that they had — as best they could — resolved their differences. "It's always worse during the winter. The nights get longer and the waiting that much harder."

Runaway welcomed the man's company. "How long will we wait for the others, Jonathan?" He rubbed at a sore spot in his leg, just above his knee.

Cooper shrugged, moving out of the doorway to where he had laid his knapsack. "Our people in Marion weren't sure when they could get our freight here." He shook his head. "We're close to the Kentucky line. Too close." The man found his tobacco and pared off a small chunk. He offered a similar piece to the boy.

Runaway sat down on his haunches, taking the tobacco. "Rebecca would scold you proper if she knew that you were using this stuff."

Jonathan hunkered down beside the boy. "Are you going to tell?"

Runaway pretended to be considering the question. "Maybe," he teased. "When we get home," the word sounded good, "maybe I'll have to 'fess right up…"

Cooper grabbed the younger man's collar, feeling play- ful. "You make sure when you tell on me you 'fess up to your own vices!" He cuffed the boy's ears. "I want you to think real hard about what Rebecca will say when you tell her how you let that little old man," he nodded toward the far corner, to the small figure that huddled there, "take away all your money with his crooked dice!" He tempered the rebuke with a smile. "Rebecca has a powerful dislike for gambling, Runaway, worse even than what she feels about this." He tapped the bulge at his cheek.

Runaway laughed softly. He raised his hands in a gesture of surrender. "If you don't mention the dice, I won't mention the tobacco."

Cooper nodded. He was quiet a moment, his mood changing as he became more pensive. "I'm going to try and sleep for a bit." The laughter was completely gone from the man's voice. He stared out into the black night, his jaws working. And then he rolled his shoulders. "You stay awake, son, wide awake." He leaned back against the wall, sliding down to rest on his heels and promptly fell asleep.

Runaway was on his feet again. He had sensed Cooper's uneasiness even before the man hinted that there might be something wrong. They had been followed for a time the day before — how close, Runaway wasn't sure — but he had felt a presence. And now he knew that Cooper had felt it, too.

Something was missing. The boy rubbed at the prickly sensation at the back of his neck, trying to fit the pieces together. And then he realized what was wrong. There was no noise, no night sounds from the woods beyond the clearing that fronted the barnyard. He reached out to where Cooper was sleeping, gently shaking the man awake.

Cooper bolted upright, his hand tightening around the carbine that lay across his knees. He canted his head, listening and then nodded at the boy. Together, they silently made their way to the small side door.

Runaway peered into the darkness of the farmyard, straining to hear. He was aware of the sound of his own breathing and that of his companion. Then, in unison, they were aware of the other noise, the quiet whisper of men moving in the pine grove beyond the fence.

Cooper moved closer to the boy. He held up his hand,

two fingers forming a "V", and then pointed to the row of trees. Shoulder to shoulder with the younger man, he finally spoke. The words were whisper quiet and Runaway had to strain to hear. "Two, I think; ten — maybe fifteen yards out."

Runaway's mouth was dry and the words came louder than he intended. "The same ones that were behind us yesterday, when we crossed the river?"

"Could be," Cooper exhaled. The darkness hid his smile. *He feels them, too,* he thought silently, feeling a pride in the things the boy had learned in the time they had been together on the road. "I don't think they are catchers," he observed. "Copperheads, most likely, looking to stop our people from keeping the line open." He reached into his pocket and withdrew a bandana, using the cloth to wipe a thin trail of tobacco juice from his chin. "I can't let them go, Runaway," he said softly.

Runaway looked into the man's face, searching for the meaning of his words. There had never been any real trouble before, nothing they couldn't buy or bluff their way out of. There had been delays, but never any trouble.

Cooper knew he needed to explain. He reached out, touching Runaway's arm. "We've got to stop them," he said. "If they stay with us, if they keep following us along the line, they'll know every station on the route, every conductor." He shook his head when the boy tried to speak and reached into the front pocket of his long coat. Without speaking, he pressed the sheathed knife into the younger man's hand. "Stay behind me."

Runaway followed the man into the night, understanding for the first time the moccasins Cooper had given him to wear earlier that morning. They moved swiftly and silently across the straw-littered barnyard, carefully keeping to the shadows and avoiding the moonlight.

It seemed like forever before they reached the first row of pines, Cooper pausing to wait until the boy caught up with him. He pressed his fingers to his lips, using gestures to show that they would separate and circle around and behind the pines, behind their pursuers.

The boy did as he was instructed, moving into the pitch blackness beneath the trees, welcoming the soft cushion of pine needles beneath his feet. He could hear the muffled sound of horses and the frightened whispering of a voice trying to silence them.

The man had his back to Runaway. He was alone with the horses, craning forward to stare into the black emptiness beyond the tree line. There was sound, the noise of a large animal running through the woods, and then an unnatural, eerie silence.

Runaway knew he could wait no longer. He moved from his hiding place and charged the man's back, his hand quickly covering the man's mouth. Instinctively — filled with a fear for his own preservation — he plunged the knife into the softness below the man's ribs. They fell to the ground together, and he felt the sudden warmth of the man's blood against his belly. Runaway rolled away from the man. He laid on the ground, breathing hard, the blood on his stomach growing cold.

The wounded man was trying to rise. He called out, "Oh, God…", and then rolled on to his side, suddenly face to face with his attacker.

Runaway found himself staring into a countenance made paler by a sudden break in the clouds. A single beam of moonlight seemed to focus on the upturned face, giving the fair skin an unearthly radiance that seemed to grow in intensity. Unable to help himself, Runaway scrambled to his feet and backed away, watching as the heat from the body formed a vapor that was lifting upwards, as if the soul were actually leaving the mortal remains. It was then Runaway realized that this was no man. It was a boy, *a smooth-cheeked, adolescent boy*.

Suddenly, the boy reached out, his fingers clawing at the air in front of Runaway. "Help me," he begged. *"Please help me!!"*

Runaway dropped to his knees. He moved to where the boy lay, reaching out to touch his face. The child was dying, his skin growing cold. He shook as if chilled by some icy wind and there was a strange bubbly sound in his throat, his chest. He tried to talk again, to call out. The words finally came. "Mama ... *Mama-a-a."*

Runaway stood up, feeling sick inside. He had killed before. The big field boss he had beaten to death with the hoe, the first time he ran away. But this was different. He had hated the first one, hated him with everything that was inside him. He had even taken pleasure in the killing, enjoying the overwhelming sense of power that had filled him.

He found no joy in this death. He had killed a boy no older than he, a boy who had cried out for his mother like any child cries out when they are left alone in the dark.

"It's going to be all right, boy." Cooper was beside him now. "There were two others," he said. He felt the boy tense under his touch, felt the shudder that coursed through the youth's long frame. "Don't think about it, Runaway. Not now." The next words came slowly. "There'll be time later, in your dreams..." he let the words fade into nothingness, sorry had had said them. Avoiding Runaway eyes, he bent down on one knee. He pulled the knife from the dead boy's back and was wiping the blade clean with a clump of long grass. Finished, he stood up. He handed the knife back to Runaway.

The young man hesitated and then took the blade. This had been a test, he realized, a way for Cooper to judge if he was really ready to do all of the things that would be required of him if their work was to continue.

He also knew now what Cooper's real job with the Underground Railroad was. Cooper was more than a conductor. He was the man who took the jobs that the others could not or would not do. He was the man who went deep into the south to bring out those who had been left behind.

Cooper's arm was lying across the younger man's shoulders, something calm and reassuring in his touch. "The price of freedom comes high, son. Yours. Mine. Any man's." He nodded to where the dead boy lay. "You did what you had to do."

Runaway placed the knife he had been holding into its sheath and fastened it to his belt. He knew now that, if he had to, he would kill again.

He knew also that he would never again take pleasure in killing.

Chapter 9

Elisha Montgomery stood in the rubble of the burned barn, the fingers of his left hand nervously working the blunted stub at his right shoulder. His face was a deep red, burning with the anger that was smoldering within him. The niggers had done this. They had torched the barns and the squalid cabins along slave row, chanting and singing as they wreaked their own mad havoc. "Emancipation. Emancipation!!"

It had started with the disgruntled rumblings among the house niggers. They had heard the old man — Elisha's uncle — ranting drunkenly about Lincoln and the "goddamned abolitionists". *"He's part nigger, 'Lish',"* the old fool babbled. *"Ever'body in Kentucky knows his father had a nigger mammy!"* The old man kept fueling his words with the corn liquor that was now his sustenance. *"That's how come for him to free the slaves. He's part nigger!"* And then the drunken old fool passed out on the parlor floor, laying in the filth of his own vomit, wallowing in it.

That was when Elisha killed him, sick of the way the old man — like his own father — was squandering away his fortune and land. Coldly, without any forethought, before it was all gone, Elisha picked up the poker from beside the fireplace, and — with the same short chop he would have used to kill a rabbit — broke the old man's neck.

He fell, Elisha said afterward, when the sheriff came. *He was drunk and he fell.* And no one doubted him.

The slaves ran that same night after they set fire to the things that now — by right of inheritance — belonged to Elisha. *What little was left.*

Montgomery stood surveying his charred kingdom. He had coveted this land a long time. There was self-sufficiency here, self-sufficiency in the silt-rich earth that topped the many fields and in the slaves that worked them. Self-sufficiency and wealth, enough wealth to last a man's lifetime.

But not without the slaves, not without their labor. Elisha rubbed at the atrophied nub again. It had started with Charlotte, all his bad luck. With Charlotte and the runaway who had taken her. Montgomery's gaze shifted to the northern horizon. Charlotte was dead, food for the rutting, wild pigs he had spooked when he shot her. But the boy, the boy and the others who had just run… They were still out there. Somewhere, beyond the river, they were still out there.

He was going to find them, all of them. And he was going to bring them back. This was the Confederacy, and here — in Kentucky — there would be no Emancipation. Not on his land. He'd see them dead first, all of them. *He would see them dead.*

***

"My God, Jonathan! How…!?" Runaway tried to move into the street for a closer look and found his way barred by Cooper's outstretched arm. January 1st had come and gone and Emancipation was now the law.

Cooper shoved the boy behind him, his eyes on the slave coffle. "Because Emancipation isn't the law, at least not here." They were in a small, pro-southern village less than five miles from the Kentucky line. He kept his eyes on the long line of slaves. It was as if the past — his past — had returned to haunt him. This was how he had brought slaves into port, took them to the auction block. Long lines of men, women and children, bound together with heavy neck yokes that scraped and slivered the skin, iron shackles banding their ankles. He remembered the sound, the shuffling and rattling as they moved. *Barefoot*, he saw. *It was mid-January and they were barefoot.* He turned his gaze to the mounted men that were guarding the coffle. They were armed, exceedingly well-armed, carrying carbines and long rifles in their saddle scabbards, and sidearms in their belts. Each man wore two bandoliers strapped across their chests, enough ammunition to supply a small army.

There was a sudden *whoosh* at Cooper's back and the sucking rush of cool air against his neck as Runaway inhaled sharply. Jonathan spoke without turning around, his eyes still on the men. "What's wrong?"

Runaway was trembling, but not in fear. "Montgomery," he hissed. "The one-armed man; that's Elisha Montgomery."

Cooper had chosen this moment to smoke his pipe. He shifted his weight when he felt the boy bolt forward, blocking the way. "Stay put," he ordered, his voice soft. "Just stay where you are."

Runaway was directly behind Cooper, so close that their bodies seemed conjoined. "He killed Charlotte," he murmured. "Dammit! He killed Charlotte!"

Cooper turned, grabbing the boy's arm, his fingers digging into the muscle above the elbow. He pulled him along, moving down the walkway, his steps measured. "We're here to find out what happened to our people, to find out why no one was waiting for us at the last station." Jonathan kept his voice low, weaving in and out among the people on the sidewalk, the boy still in tow. He stepped down into the street, pausing as a wagon rumbled by in front of them, and then continuing on his way, heading for the boarding house.

Runaway reached out in a futile attempt to pry the man's fingers from his arm. He cursed, fighting the man's grip. "Didn't you hear me?" he rasped. "He killed Charlotte!"

Cooper pulled the boy into the narrow alley beside the lodging house. He slammed the youth against the rough siding, holding him. "I heard you," he answered. "The way our luck's been running, the whole damned town heard you!" Angry at the boy's carelessness, he shook him. "You can't do anything, Runaway." He lifted his hands away from the boy's shoulders, his palms flat against the side of the building, the youth between his stiff arms. His breathing had returned to normal and the red flush at his neck was gradually fading. "You can't *change* anything. The best we can hope for is to keep him from killing anyone else.

"From killing us!"

Runaway stood stock still, the anger leaving him. "You're going to try and take the slaves..." He saw from the man's face that he had guessed right. He began shaking his head, rocking it back and forth against the wall at his back. "You can't do it, Jonathan." He pushed himself away from the wall, ducking under the man's arms, subdued. "There's no way you can do it!"

"I can try." Cooper said, more to himself than to the boy. "*We* can try." He waved his hand at the boy, signaling for him to follow, and headed out of the alley and back into the main street. His boots thumped across the plank boardwalk.

Runaway was a full pace behind Cooper, the proper distance for a tote-and-fetch boy, his gaze on the ground. It was the way they always walked when they were in a strange town this far south, among people they did not know. He chose his words carefully, keeping them soft, timing them to the passing traffic. "You can't do it," he said again, holding his silence as a man approached them. He kept quiet until the stranger passed and was well behind them. "And the others…" A woman was approaching them, dragging her toddler beside her. "What about the others…"

Cooper turned into the gabled doorway that fronted the modest boarding house. He didn't answer the boy, just led the way to their room, pausing on the landing to stare down the long hallway on the second floor. Reaching back, he touched the boy's sleeve, pointing down the passageway to the door of their room. His pace increased and he led the way to the door, bending down.

There was a basket in front of the door, a small wicker basket. Nine brown shelled eggs nested inside, resting on a neatly folded red napkin. Cooper bent down, picking up the parcel, his brow knotting. Without saying anything, he unlocked the door and went inside, standing aside as Runaway joined him.

"Eggs." Runaway took the basket, puzzled. He looked up at Cooper. "Who would bring us eggs?"

Cooper was at the window, peering out into the street. He closed the curtains, going back to where the boy stood. "Friends," he answered. "Rebecca's Friends." He was talking about the Quakers.

Runaway still didn't understand. There was some

significance in this gift. He held the basket up again, "I don't..."

"The nine eggs," Cooper picked one up, holding it between his thumb and forefinger "mean there are nine Negroes." He replaced the egg, running his fingers over the others. They were uniform in color, but not in size, three pullet eggs in the center. "Six adults, three children." He worked the red napkin loose from the bottom of the basket. "The red cloth means that there has been trouble." He unfolded the cloth, catching the piece of paper that had been concealed among the folds. It looked like a printed advertisement, a flyer that would be passed out by any merchant promoting his goods.

Runaway watched as Cooper took the paper over to the bedside table. A corner room, the area was well lighted, windows on the two outer walls, and yet Jonathan was lighting the kerosene lantern. He lifted the globe, adjusting the wick until there was just a small flame. And then he sat the chimney glass on the table, manipulating the paper and careful to keep it the proper distance from the flickering wick.

Runaway could see the writing on the paper now. It appeared typeset, the letters well-spaced, nothing more than a polite note of welcome from the church elders and an invitation to attend the weekend service.

Then Cooper did a strange thing. It appeared for a moment that he was going to burn the note. He held it over the small flame, keeping the sheet flat and rigid as he moved it slowly back and forth. More letters began to appear, hand printed along the generous margins bordering the centered type. Runaway moved closer, mouthing the words as the message became visible: *Freight held up at station in Cairo; train derailed by flooding. Conductor sick with ague;*

station-master succumbed Saturday a.m., lead poisoning.
Three packages missing. Rerouting traffic through Herrin.

Cooper swore; vehemently. He wadded the note up in his fist, his hand hovering for a time above the flame. Herrin. Almost forty miles north of where they were now. Forty miles traveling at night, on foot. "You saw?" he asked, opening his palm to expose the crumpled paper.

Runaway nodded. "What does it mean?" He took the note, smoothing it out on the table.

"They were waylaid, ambushed." Cooper picked up the note from the table. He put the paper to the flame, rotating the sheet until there was nothing but ash. Then he put the glass back on the lantern and extinguished the flame. "The conductor was injured and the station-master..." he hesitated, "...the station-master was shot." He went to the chiffonier on the far wall, opening the doors. "They lost three of the passengers they were transporting," he took out the heavy carpetbag that contained their clothing and dug deep inside. When he withdrew his hand, he was holding a small leather pouch. "I want you to stay here, Runaway." He nodded at the room, the bed. "I want you to stay right here until I get back."

The boy watched as Cooper shoved the pouch into the inside pocket of his coat. Cooper never went anywhere that Runaway had not been able to go with him. Not once, not in all the long months they had been traveling together. Sometimes they traveled as equals; when necessary, as slave and master, but always together. "No." The refusal was complete.

Cooper was already at the door. He half-turned, his hand on the knob. "I have some things I have to do before we can leave here, some things I need to get, and some people I need to see. I don't want to take the chance that

Montgomery might see you."

Runaway was shaking his head. "It's been a long time," he said evenly. He swept a hand down the length of his body. "I've grown considerably since the last time he saw me. I've changed; enough that he won't know me." He didn't know who he was trying to convince, Cooper or himself.

Cooper canted his head, studying the boy's face. "Not enough," he said quietly, "and not here," he tapped his own chest with a single finger, at a spot right over his heart. "I won't have you doing anything foolish, just because you suddenly feel a need to get even."

Runaway crossed the floor. "I can take care of myself, Jonathan!" he said, his voice rising. He thumped his chest, feeling cock-sure of himself. "I know you're going to try and find a way to take those slaves from Montgomery, from his men.

"I'm going with you!" he declared stubbornly.

Cooper's face tensed, his mouth forming a tight line. He was thinking of his son now, and the fight that had occurred the first time the young boy had tried to leave the farm to enlist. "No," he breathed. "You're going to stay here, right here!" When it was clear the boy wasn't listening, he moved. He slapped the youth hard, an open-handed blow that came suddenly and unexpectedly. "I mean it, son," he said quietly.

Runaway backed up a full pace, his fingers on his burning cheek, a sore burning in his throat as he blinked back the tears. In all the time he had been with Jonathan and Rebecca, not once had either one of them raised a hand to him. And now Jonathan had struck him, slapped his face much as he would have struck a small child for speaking out of turn. The boy's lower lip trembled. *A baby. He's treating me like some snot-nosed baby!*

Cooper swept the boy with a long, disapproving stare, his eyes as cold as his voice. "You're not to leave this room," he ordered. "I don't want to lock you in, Runaway," he lifted his hand, displaying the key, "but I will. If that's what it takes, I will."

Runaway turned his back on the man, his pride smarting just as intensely as his left cheek. "I'll stay," he whispered.

***

Cooper spent the afternoon bird-dogging Montgomery's tracks. He had learned much during their first brief encounter on the street when Runaway had been at his back. The men who were with Montgomery were professional catchers, mercenaries and profiteers selling their services to the highest bidder, men who served no cause other than their own.

There were other things he had learned. Montgomery was not heading south. He was moving northward, looking for runaway slaves fleeing in premature anticipation of the promised Emancipation, slaves he had owned and many that he did not. With no one to oppose him, he was taking every Negro he encountered, man, woman or child.

Cooper made one stop before he returned to the boarding house. He headed for a shop on the main street, pausing to examine the sign that hung above the door. Squaring his shoulders, he went inside.

***

Runaway was lying on the bed when Jonathan returned to the room. It was dark, and the young man had not bothered to light the lantern, choosing instead to brood in the black silence that matched his mood. He heard Jonathan's footsteps, and the awkward sound of the man struggling with the door and then a dull *thunk* as something fell on the carpeted floor. Still, the youth did not rise.

Cooper entered the room, his arms full. He kicked the door shut. "I need some light, Runaway," he said softly.

The boy didn't respond verbally. There was a soft creaking as he pivoted and swung off the bed and then the noise of glass scraping against metal. Cooper caught the scent of and sound of a sulphur-tipped match being struck, saw a brief flicker of light, and then more flame as the kerosene-soaked wick ignited.

Cooper crossed the room to the bed, dumping his packages out on the multi-colored patchwork quilt. He stood back, waving his hand at the collection of handguns. "Pick one," he said nodding at the youth.

Runaway was still angry over their earlier confrontation. He hesitated, his curiosity getting the best of him. And then he returned to the bed, fingering the cold metal that gleamed beneath the pale light of the dim lantern. The collection of firearms was formidable. The boy counted a total of eight pistols. He reached out, watching Cooper's face as he picked up each piece and hefted them against his flat palm. He continued sorting through the weapons until he picked up a Smith & Wesson .32 caliber rimfire revolver.

Cooper smiled and nodded his approval, opening his coat at the waist to expose a matching pistol. "Good," he breathed. He reached out, digging into the pile of boxes. "Cartridges," he said. He pulled his pistol from its holster, opening the chamber to expose the cylinder. Carefully, he loaded the piece, holding the pistol so the boy could see. "The others," he nodded at the assembled arms still on the bed, "are cap and ball pistols. I'll show you how to load them later; how to handle them." Finished, he shoved his revolver back into his belt.

"You're taking our people to Herrin, Runaway. You're going to take them to freedom."

***

They ate their supper in the room, Cooper trying hard to keep up a façade of good-humored banter throughout the meal. The forced joviality had the opposite effect of what he had hoped. Runaway's fears surfaced a half dozen times before they were finished eating, his fears and the old self-doubts. "I can't do this," he murmured.

Cooper refused to listen. He continued the lessons he had begun earlier that evening. One by one, he reviewed the different weapons, concentrating on the intricate workings of the cap and ball pistols. "There will be two other men with you, farmers, most likely. They'll have their own rifles with them, but they may need the pistols." He picked up one of the cap and ball Spencers. "I want the others armed for defense, Runaway, not for attack." It was difficult trying to explain the workings of the firearms without an opportunity to actually fire the pieces.

"Your pistol," he said, taking the .32. "You'll feel a slight kick — a recoil — when you fire like striking an anvil with small hammer. It will be that kind of feeling, a jolt immediately after you fire. You have to remember that; anticipate it."

Runaway was fascinated with the weapons, with the sense of power he seemed to draw from the now familiar feel of the cold steel. He felt nine feet tall and growing.

Cooper sensed the change in the boy, his eyes narrowing as he watched the youth handling the pistol. He reached out, taking the weapon for the second time. He almost had to pry the thing from the boy's fingers. "Montgomery," he surmised, studying the boy's face. "You're thinking of Montgomery."

Runaway turned away before answering. "No," he said quickly, too quickly. He stared at the far wall, reconsidering. "I was thinking about the things he did," he said. It wasn't a total lie. He *was* thinking of the man's deeds as much as he was thinking of the physical being that was Montgomery. There was something sinister in the man, evil, the kind of evil that allowed him to murder not only the woman who had borne him a son and a daughter but to allow those children to die as well.

Cooper was packing the weapons away, carefully wrapping them in individual oilcloth packets that would be easy to conceal. "It's not your place to pass judgment, Runaway. Not on me and not on Montgomery."

Runaway's head snapped up, his eyes meeting Cooper's. "I'll kill him," he said finally. "If I get a chance, I'll kill him."

Cooper shook his head, a sadness in him. "You'll take our people to Herrin," he breathed. "You'll stay with them there and wait for me.

"Two days," he finished. "You wait for me for two days," he shook his head when the boy tried to speak. "If I'm not there, you take them on to the station at Sesser. There'll be another conductor waiting for you." Cooper took a map from his pocket and shoved it into the boy's hands. "Two days," he reminded the youth. "No more, no less."

Runaway took the chart, his eyes on the floor. There was nothing he could say, no argument he could offer.

Not any argument that he would win. Cooper had made up his mind, had already decided what he must do. *Alone.* Runaway tried again. "Jonathan…"

Cooper shook his head. He was disappointed in the boy and that disappointment showed in his face, his silence.

They spent the rest of the evening in total quiet, waiting for darkness. Then, together, they hiked the small footpath leading to the edge of town. There was no moon this night, just the white mist of their breath on the cold air and the sound of their breathing. Cooper tugged at the boy's sleeve as they entered the woods, reaching out in the darkness to grope for the younger man's hand. "God go with you, son," he said softly, his fingers closing around Runaway's wrist, tightening briefly, then letting go.

Runaway watched as Cooper disappeared into the darkness, his footsteps fading into the night. It wasn't until Cooper was gone that he realized just how often in the past few weeks the man had called him *son*. "Take care, Jonathan," he whispered. He wished he had said the words aloud and that Cooper had heard them.

Chapter 10

Cooper sat alone in the dark corner of the long, narrow room, his eyes watching the coming and going of the townsmen. He could tell by the familiarity and the banter which were the regular customers, farmers, mostly, and later, the merchants from the many small stores that lined the main street of the small village.

The tavern was well suited to Cooper's needs. He could observe the mood of the people, eavesdrop on their lubricated conversations. *Secessionists*, he mused. In this place, among their peers, they felt safe discussing opinions and beliefs that would be considered treason further north.

The loyalties of these people were firmly entrenched. The fact that Lincoln was from Illinois — that he had been, like them, born and reared in Kentucky — did not impress them. He was, in their opinion, the traitor. The man had betrayed his southern brethren, destroyed the Union, and was guilty of spilling southern blood.

Because of the niggers. The word was used liberally in the place. The men discussed niggers, Lincoln and abolitionists in one breath and with the same degree of contempt. Cooper held his place and his silence, content simply to observe. *Slavery,* he knew, *might have been the rallying call of the War, but the true issue was states' rights.*

Observe and wait. Cooper shifted in his chair. He had spent the afternoon well, buying additional arms and even more information. He did these things cautiously, assimilating all that he had learned.

Montgomery would be here soon. That much Cooper had learned from his inquiries. It has become a ritual with the man. He had come to the village hunting his own fugitive slaves, spreading the word he would pay well for his runaways, as well as any other Negro suspect in the eyes the already biased townsmen.

He kept his captured Negroes in the livery, adding to the coffle as the townspeople came forward with information regarding any black unfortunate enough to have garnered special attention. Some townsmen, fearing that Emancipation would become a reality throughout Illinois if the North won the War, brought their slaves, feeling smug as they took Montgomery's money.

They were the clever ones, the merchants and farms who kept niggers openly in a state that had entered the Union as free. '*Indentured servants*', they called them, claiming the slaves were simply working to pay off debts and thereby purchase their freedom.

The debts, of course (which often never existed), were never repaid, no matter how long or how hard the blacks worked.

Cooper toyed with the glass of warm beer, staring into the briny foam, seeing his reflection in the larger bubbles. *Strange,* he mused, *how a man could cajole himself into believing that he was above the law, that the ordinary rules of civilized behavior did not apply to his own circumstances.*

He had been that way in the beginning. Bending the laws regarding the transport of slaves as it suited him. He openly defied the British and the Americans to sail his slave ship, delivering its cargo of human flesh to ports in the Deep South and Mexico under the cover of darkness. *Always in darkness, like some night crawling vermin.*

He had done it all; breaking the law, lying to Rebecca. Spending three months out of the year hiding inland on their farm, pretending that there was nothing wrong in the things he had done, the things he had continued to do. For three months, he was the perfect husband, the ideal father. *The good Christian.* No Quaker, certainly, but a God-fearing, good and dutiful family man.

Just as he had remained the good and dutiful ship's captain. *Slaver,* he reminded himself. A man who loved the sea, who loved the God-like power the sea gave him, the power of life and death, the right to choose who would live, and who would die. *What cargo he would carry, and why.*

For revenge, at first; after his father was murdered. That was why he had begun slaving, to avenge his father's death and to redeem his own lost childhood. But later, a short time later, it was for the money, just the money. Cooper inhaled, a tightness in his chest, a feeling that the air was growing sparse, and that the walls of the room were closing in about him. He closed his eyes, his hand rubbing at the sharp pain across his forehead. He was remembering the closeness — the putrid stench — below the decks of his ship. The sea of brown faces; brown bodies chained — stacked — into the narrow confines in the darkness of the ship's hold. *Hell,* he thought, *a living hell of his making.*

There was a brief pause in the muted conversations, and then the voices resumed. Cooper opened his eyes, staring into the smoke-filled room, his attention on the man that had just entered. Montgomery. He watched as the man crossed the room, marked the arrogance and sureness with which he moved. He had been like that once. Sure of himself, of his divine right to be superior to anyone he deemed different from himself.

It seemed so long ago sometimes, almost as if the memories he had were remembrances of some other man in some other time, a different man capable of great acts of cruelty. *Just like Montgomery.*

Cooper shook the dark thoughts from his head. This was his last trip. He was going to take the slaves that Montgomery had captured — the slaves he had purchased — and carry them north to freedom. And then he was going to find Runaway and go home. Both of them, back to the farm, back to Rebecca.

He stood up, empty glass in hand, and began to weave through the growing crowd of people. Montgomery was at the long bar, facing the door, a cat-like awareness about him. Cooper approached the bar, coming up on Montgomery's right side. Both hands in plain sight, he set his glass down on the bar and signaled for a refill. With his left hand, he dug into his vest pocket for the pouch that contained the remainder of his tobacco. The small knife blade flashed blue-white in the dim lantern light as he cut off a small wad. He reached out, offering the chaw to the man at his left side. "You buy niggers?" he breathed, keeping his tone conversational, private.

Montgomery hesitated, accepting the tobacco. "I buy niggers," he answered.

"Twenty?" Cooper asked, working his chew into the side of his mouth. He watched Montgomery covertly, out of the corner of his eye.

Elisha's mouth dropped open and he quit working the

tobacco. A small stream of juice dribbled down the side of his mouth, and he brushed it away with the back of his hand. "Where?" he demanded, unable to conceal the eagerness in his voice.

Cooper was more successful suppressing the smile that tugged at the corner of his mouth. "I can show you," he said. "If the price is right, I can take you to them."

Montgomery turned around, still not looking at Cooper directly. He chose instead to survey the man's reflection in the gilt-framed mirror that hung behind the bar. "I've seen you before," he said finally.

Cooper nodded. "I've been around. I was in front of the mercantile when you and your men brought the coffle into town for water."

Montgomery signaled the barkeep and ordered a shot of rye. "You could have called out to me then," he said. He stroked his chin, scratching at the stubble on his neck.

Cooper shook his head. "I'm a stranger here," he said truthfully. "I'm not about to call attention to myself until I know the climate." He took a long drink of his beer. "Man in my business has to be careful." He smiled. "For all I know you could be an Abolitionist, pretending to be a slaver when what you're really doing is smuggling slaves north."

Montgomery turned suddenly, facing Cooper fully. He snorted. "Is that what you found out?" he asked. He made no attempt to hide the sarcasm. "All that time you spent asking questions about me, about where I come from?" He reached out, his arched forefinger probing under Cooper's heavy coat to tap the butt of Cooper's pistol. "Buying this?"

Cooper met the man's gaze fully, a half smile touching his lips. "This," he brushed Montgomery's hand away from the weapon, "and others." There was no point in lying. He was aware that Montgomery had been making inquiries about him as well. His smile grew. The time for lying was now. "Hard to come by a decent piece anymore, at least south of here." He knew from Montgomery's raised eyebrow that the man understood his meaning. "You buy and sell slaves; I buy and sell weapons." He lifted his glass as if in a toast. "To the Confederacy," he said, nodding at Montgomery's full glass.

Elisha picked up his drink. "To the Confederacy," he echoed.

***

Her name was Sally. Runaway had learned that during their nighttime trek toward Herrin. She didn't know her age or the name of the place she had come from. Only that the others had run and she had simply followed after them.

She had a way of speaking that made Runaway uncomfortable, impatient. Her speech pattern was the same as the field hands Runaway had known, filled with the dialects and the hard to understand slurring of words and letters. *Norf*, he thought. All of her *ths* came out like *fs*. Once she had begun talking to him, she had prattled on, incessantly, and Runaway was constantly asking her to talk slower, to repeat herself. Over and over again, until he would throw up his hands in despair and leave her to the others, stomping off into the darkness ahead of them. She would run after him then, dogging his steps, asking a hundred questions, but never waiting for the answers.

She had also been filthy. In a fit of anger, at one of their overnight stops in a place where they had been provided soap and water and a chance for clean clothes, Runaway had plunged her neck deep into a rain barrel, refusing to let her out until she had scrubbed herself and discarded her rags.

That was when he first realized she was with child. With absolutely no shame or modesty, she had climbed stark naked out of the rain barrel, shaking herself like a dog until he had covered her with a blanket and helped her to dry. She had seen the expression on his face and laughed at what she thought was embarrassment on his part. And then she told him about how she had been chosen — as if it was something special — to mate with her owner's son and '*make massa mo' babies*'.

Her acceptance that she could be used that way angered Runaway. It also was — for him — one more indication that she was truly ignorant and destined by choice to stay that way.

What really tore at Runaway was the fact that the girl was a bitter reminder of Charlotte, Charlotte and Montgomery. Runaway temporarily consoled himself with the thought that Charlotte, at least, had fooled herself into thinking that Elisha had cared for her and would grant her freedom. Charlotte had been deceived, he thought. But Sally, Sally had allowed herself to be used, had accepted the idea that she was a thing, a possession. In her stupidity (and stupidity is what Runaway considered it) she had been willing to bring forth the child of a free white man with the full knowledge that — because she was black — the child would be considered black. *And a black child was a slave child.*

Runaway hated that, that the girl took pride in what she had done. Worse, that she had absolutely no shame.

So he ignored her. Or tried.

He took her, the first night at the station in Herrin, after she had bathed. There was nothing tender in him or in the way he used her. She was simply there, sleeping next to him, unaware of his sudden midnight arousal. He satisfied himself, his needs, and then turned his back on her, paying no attention to her quiet sobs. It didn't matter that he had hurt her, had caused her pain. *She's used to it*, he thought, quieting the twinge of conscience that threatened to touch him. *It's what she expected.*

What she deserves. He rolled over on his stomach then and fell asleep.

***

Cooper had learned much in his time with Montgomery. It had been Elisha who had taken the slaves at Cairo and who had engineered the raid on the station there, Elisha and the men who were with him.

They boasted about it, in the evening beside their fire. Boasted about how they had learned from informers that the underground railroad was again actively taking and hiding runaway slaves, opening up the same routes that had been so frequently used in the 1830s and '40s. *Abolitionists*, the men scoffed. Pious old men and addled women who expressed their radical beliefs in freed slaves and suffrage for women. The men snorted and hooted, fueling their ridicule with the bottles of corn liquor Montgomery had supplied. Freeing the slaves made about as much sense as allowing a woman to vote, they reasoned. And what kind of fool would ever allow a woman a voice in any government!

In truth, these men had no political allegiances, Cooper discovered. They would sell their loyalty and services to the anti-slave faction as quickly as they had already sold them to Montgomery.

Cooper used that knowledge. He worked with the men, leading them on a circuitous route towards Herrin. There were four others with Montgomery, two that watched his back.

The other two — the ones who were the most quiet, the most cognizant of their ever-changing surroundings — watched their own backs. It was these two that Cooper paid to join him. It had been relatively easy. *I know what he's paying you,* Cooper told them. *And I know how he's paying you.* The men had all accepted Confederate paper. *I'll pay you in gold,* he bargained, understanding the men and their reasoning. *Half now, half when we reach Herrin.* Gold was good no matter who won the War.

It was a dangerous game, one that Jonathon had played many times, and he played it well. He kept himself aloof from the others, watching them, watching all of them.

Before this was over, he would have all of the fugitive slaves with him and on their way North. They would all come together at Herrin. The slaves Montgomery had taken — fifteen runaways from his own plantation, three from the ambush at Cairo, and five unfortunates taken along the way — the nine delayed passengers that Montgomery had failed to take, and the dozen he had sent on ahead with Runaway. *Forty-four,* Cooper tallied mentally.

He had been master of his own ship for three years. In that time he had successfully transported three hundred thirteen slaves.

He had been a full-time conductor on the Underground Railroad for five years. And for the first time in all those long years, he had finally balanced the scale, with some to spare.

At least as much as he was able. He could never redeem the one hundred thirteen slaves he had put over the side in the Gulf of Mexico no matter how hard or how long he tried. He'd done what he could do and there was no more.

He was getting too old for this. Old and tired. He'd lost his son, and — for a time — had only a nodding acquaintance with his daughters. He was going to rest after this trip. He would continue his work with the underground and the abolitionists as long as his services were needed but not as a conductor.

A station master, he thought. He and Rebecca had done well enough on the farm that they had been able to purchase a second, smaller place, closer to the river. He would use that place as a way station. It would be safe far enough away from the War and among the Friends.

He could stay home, still do his work and stay home. No more long separations from Rebecca and the girls. *Home.* He never tired of saying the word, of hearing it.

Home.

***

Two days, Runaway and the other had been in Herrin for two days. Resting, enjoying the luxury of hot meals and warm water for their aching feet.

Runaway stood in the kitchen, a mug of hot tea in his hand. The station master, Mr. Outerbridge, was with him, a compact man who in spite of his bookish demeanor and age (Runaway assumed him to be in his fifties) was in remarkable physical shape. He had salt and pepper hair, closely cropped, and sepia-colored skin and eyes that betrayed his mixed heritage.

The existing edicts regarding miscegenation — the laws prohibiting marriage between persons of different races — had limited him as a youth until his parents sent him to Europe to be educated. He had returned to the country of his birth when he was twenty-one, to a society that considered him his mother's son and a man of color and yet he had chosen to stay. The fact that his father had left him a substantial inheritance helped and he had no illusions regarding the fact that it was his fortune that guaranteed his acceptance in a community that relied on his benevolence. He owned the local bank as well as the general store and the mill.

It was not wealth, but the man's obvious self esteem and his manner of speaking that intrigued Runaway, the quiet way of talking that made all those around him lean closer to hear and give undivided attention to his words. This was a truly well-educated man who read the classics and understood them. *Oxford*, he told Runaway. He had spent two years in England, studying literature. *Chaucer. Bede. Shakespeare.*

He had given Runaway a copy of *Othello*. The boy read it, with some difficulty, marveling at the story of a black man functioning — growing rich — in a white world. The tragic ending did not matter to the youth or Othello's manipulation by Iago. It was the place he had attained, the social stature that the Moor had achieved.

"Did you enjoy it?"

Runaway hefted the volume in his hand, one finger on the ornate, gilded leather spine. "Yes," he answered, after a time. He exchanged a look with the man. "Yes, Mr. Outerbridge."

The older man nodded, his eyes bright. "Enjoyed, but not totally comprehended?" Outerbridge took the book, studying it for a time over the top of his glasses. "Don't apologize, Runaway. The noble bard," he tapped the author's name with his forefinger, the gesture almost

loving, "was meant to be enjoyed more than be analyzed."
The smile widened and he winked. "The understanding
will come later," he promised. His mood changed and he
replaced the book on the long shelves that lined the wall
beside the fieldstone fireplace. "We've had word from
Jonathon," he said.

Runaway exhaled, relieved. He had already disobeyed
Cooper's last instruction, refusing to leave the farm after
the two-day deadline. *Just one more day*, he had told Sally
and the others that very morning. He knew that he would
have stayed longer, much longer. *As long as it took*. "He's
coming?" he asked, trying to read the man's face.

Outerbridge nodded. He took off his glasses, rubbing
at the lenses with his handkerchief. "Not here," he said.
There was the sound of shod hooves in the barnyard, many
shod hooves. Outerbridge canted his head, still cleaning
his spectacles, unconcerned. He stared across at Runaway,
as if debating his words, as if there was something that he
was working over in his mind.

Satisfied, he carefully put the wire-rimmed glasses
back on, adjusting them against the bridge of his nose.
The lenses seemed to magnify his eyes, to add intensity to
them. "There is an old homestead, just south of here. It's
abandoned now, but in the beginning — when the Railroad
first started — it was one of the larger receiving stations."
He gestured with an ambiguous wave of his hand. "Cooper
will be there," he said; "Cooper and the others."

The others. Runaway mentally parroted the old man's
final words. *Cooper and the others*. "What others?" he
asked aloud.

Outerbridge was hesitating again, measuring his answer. "Slaves," he said the word as if it left a rancid taste in
his mouth. "A man named Montgomery, four 'catchers'."

He lifted his head, staring across at the youth, his brow knotting. "Two of the men have agreed — for a price — to help Cooper with his ruse." There was a knock on the door and the old man went to the doorway without pausing in his speech. "We'll have more help," he said, opening the door. He stood aside as the other men trooped in, nodding in greeting.

They were a strange assembly. An even half dozen, ranging it seemed, from a smooth-cheeked child to a white-bearded ancient. Runaway studied them, reassessing his first judgment. There was no gradual spanning of the years. There were the very old and the very young. *The War,* he reasoned. *The fit — those in their prime — were always marched off to the wars. Cannon fodder,* he thought, remembering something that Rebecca had said to him once, during the long months when he was recovering from his sickness. "*They* (he never quite understood who *they* were) *take our sons, and turn them into cannon fodder, before they ever have a chance to really live.*"

"…he will be here tomorrow night," Outerbridge was saying. "Twenty-three fugitives, he's bringing twenty-three lost souls up from bondage." There was a great deal of passion in the man's voice.

Runaway moved closer to the table where the others were assembled. "I'm going with you," he announced, watching as the group exchanged worried glances with Outerbridge. "Cooper's my friend," he said, beginning again.

But it wasn't Cooper he was thinking of, not now. *He was thinking of Elisha Montgomery, Elisha Montgomery and all the things that had passed between them.*

Chapter 11

It had been a long night for Runaway. He rose up from his place in the hay, watching as the vapor rose from the deep hollow where he had lain. His back and shoulders ached and his mood — his temperament — was as tender as the sore spot at the base of his spine.

Outerbridge joined him at the wide barn door. He had a container of hot tea in his hand and he poured a tin cupful for the youth. "Have you told the others?" he asked.

Runaway took the cup, shaking his head. "Not everything; just that we'll be here for a bit longer." He smiled a smug smile. "They'll be all right. As long as their bellies are full, and they have a blanket to warm them; they'll be all right."

Outerbridge's back stiffened. There was something — an arrogance — in the boy's tone that offended him. "Do you consider yourself something more than the rest; something better?" he asked, his voice brittle.

Runaway felt his cheeks color. He swung his head toward the man, returning the disapproving scrutiny. It hadn't been that long ago that Jonathan had accused him of the same thing. Unable to meet the man's eyes; the power — the contempt — he saw behind the older man's eyes, he looked away. "No," he lied.

Outerbridge shook his head, making a small scolding sound with his tongue. "Your beginning was no different from theirs," he said softly. "No different from any other man or woman or child."

"No different from yours?" Runaway returned sharply. He thumped his chest with a clenched palm. "I was born a slave," he declared angrily. "A slave!!"

Outerbridge was unimpressed. He sipped his tea. "So were we all," he said cryptically, "in one fashion or another. A slave to society's rules, our passions," he took another drink, still speaking in riddles, "to our learning.

"Even to our pride," he finished, raking the boy with his eyes. He threw the remainder of his tea onto the ground, watching as the thirsty dry earth consumed its warmth. Then he flashed a wide smile, digging into his pocket. "This will make the time pass more quickly," he said. He offered the boy a tattered pamphlet, waving it impatiently when the youth didn't respond. "Take it," he ordered.

Reluctantly, Runaway did as he was told. He fingered the booklet, staring hard at Outerbridge's back, watching as the small man strode purposefully toward his house. Angry, he wadded up the pocket-sized missive, balling in his fist. He stood there for a time, hating the old man for having read him so well.

Feeling the fool, he began to wander around the yard. The sun had just begun its long climb into the morning sky and he turned his face to receive its warmth. *Twelve hours*, he calculated. Twelve hours until the rendezvous with Cooper.

With Montgomery, he reminded himself. Restless, he

began pacing; up and down in the barnyard, keeping himself between the old man in the house and the others still inside the barn. That's what he felt, deep inside; separate, apart from the rest. By choice from those still sleeping in the barn; and by…

…*by what*? He asked himself, turning to stare at the closed door of Outerbridge's home. There was something about the old man that made him feel alien strange. He swore, at Outerbridge, at the others, but mostly at himself.

***

"It's time," Outerbridge reached out to the sleeping youth, shaking him awake.

Runaway bolted upright. He had dozed off after the noon meal, falling asleep in the back of the wagon Outerbridge and the others had readied for some mysterious mission.

There was nothing unusual inside the wagon. A thin layer of fresh straw and that was all. Runaway yawned, scratching himself. When he opened his eyes, he was face to face with the eldest of the white men who had come to help. "The weapons, son," the old said. "Jonathan sent word you had weapons."

Runaway nodded dumbly. He had never understood the secret network the Railroad had for everything. Passengers, actual goods. Messages. "In the barn," he said. "I hid them in the barn."

"Good lad," the old man said, smiling his approval. He stood back from the tailgate, waiting for Runaway to join him on the ground. And then his arm was around the youth's shoulder and they were walking toward the barn. "Jonathan is bringing the slavers to us. We'll be inside the wagon, waiting for them," he said. He laughed, a deep hearty laugh that came from the very soles of his feet. "They think they are getting a wagonload of fugitives, in exchange for a fist full of silver." He shook his head. "Judas money," he said, slapping the boy's back.

Runaway led the way to the place where he had hidden the carpetbag Cooper had given him. He pulled it from behind a loose plank that divided the main stabling area from a smaller storeroom. He bent down, sitting Indian-fashion as he loosened the single, center strap. One by one, he took out the carefully wrapped packets, his fingers smoothing the slick-faced oilcloth. Seven packets. He waved his hand over them, displaying them for the old man, carefully closing the carpetbag with his free hand.

The old man sighed. He studied the packages for a time, his hands on his hips. Then he shook his head, his voice soft as he spoke. "My name is Jeremiah," he said quietly, using — as did all the others — only his first name. "I can tolerate many things in a man," he continued, reaching down to place a heavy hand on Runaway's shoulder. "Deceit is not one of those things," he finished. He waited for a time, his voice even softer when he spoke again. "There were to be eight," he said, pointing to the parcels, something accusatory in his voice.

Runaway was taken aback, slow in realizing what the older man was suggesting. Then it struck him. The old man thought he had taken one of the weapons, had *stolen* one of the weapons. "Jonathan gave me this," he said, opening his coat to display the pistol that was secured in his belt. His tone was defensive.

Jeremiah realized his mistake but he did not apologize. "Then you shall keep it," he declared. His voice softened. "Jonathan thinks highly of you, lad. I hope you will not do anything to disappoint him."

Runaway was still not sure about the older man and unsure as to how he should respond, but knowing that something was expected, he said "What does he want us to do?" He stood up.

Jeremiah pointed to the pistols. "Bring them," he ordered. He jerked a thumb toward the open door. "We'll wait until dark and then we'll go on to the meeting place." He headed back towards the wagon, hesitating until Runaway caught up with him. "Have they been fired?" he asked suddenly, his hand on the boy's arm.

"No," Runaway answered. "Jonathan said that they were to be used for defense and then only if there was a real danger of being taken." He straightened, squaring his shoulders.

The old man nodded absently, his pace increasing as if he were racing the shadows across the yard. "You may get your chance," he said, "before the night is over." Without breaking stride, the man shook his fist at the setting sun. "By God, how I wish I was young enough to be in the thick of it…" He pulled Runaway to him. "*This* war," he said, seeing the look on the boy's face. "The war Jonathan is fighting! He had no use for the other."

Runaway was taken aback by the big man's earnest wishes. A man would have to be crazy to wish himself in the middle of Jonathan's nighttime sojourns when there was no real way to know who the enemy was and who was not. Man to man conflict he could understand, a Northern soldier against his known foe, the Johnny Reb. Jonathan's battles were different, too often, one man against many.

***

Cooper led Montgomery to the clearing outside the entrance of the old stock barn. He remained mounted, waiting for the man to join him.

"You said they would be here." Montgomery came up on Cooper's left, remaining to the side and slightly behind. He wrapped the reins loosely around the stock of his sheathed carbine, freeing his left hand. Suspicious, he fingered the butt of his revolver.

"They'll come," Cooper said. He swung down from his mount, putting the animal between himself and Montgomery.

Montgomery surveyed the empty clearing, probing the darkness beyond. "You'd better hope so, friend," he said softly.

Cooper was about to respond when he heard the sound of the approaching wagon. He smiled up at Montgomery, gesturing toward the noise with his out-flung arm. "I don't make promises I can't keep."

Montgomery kneed his mount, turning the animal to face the other man. The bay gelding began to dance beneath him, feeling the man's eagerness. Elisha pulled the reins free from the carbine, jerking them hard until the animal stood still. "That's a small wagon," he said, watching Cooper's face.

"We stack them," Cooper answered, "like we did on the ships."

Montgomery smiled, his mood changing. "I knew it," he declared, relaxing. "From the way you moved, walked." He laughed, removing his hat. He mopped his brow with his shirtsleeve and replaced the worn fedora. "You were a slaver, a goddamned sea slaver!" The wariness of the past days eased. "Seized your ship, did they?" He dismounted, his back to Cooper.

Jonathan moved, coming up quickly behind Montgomery, pressing close to the man's back. "Don't move," he whispered into the man's ear. "Don't even think about moving." He shoved the barrel of his revolver into the man's back, directly against his spine. "Tell your men to bring the slaves into the clearing," he ordered. When the man hesitated, Jonathan cocked the pistol, pressing it harder into Montgomery's back. "Tell them," he hissed.

Montgomery sucked in a lungful of cold air in an effort to make himself thinner, as if it would relieve the pressure of the gun that was jammed against the small of his back. "The niggers!" he roared. "Bring the niggers in!"

Cooper nodded his silent approval. He collared the man, pulling him away from the horse. "Durham," he called. "Hill!" He watched as the two men rode into the clearing. "Now," he ordered.

"The gold," Hill answered.

"When we are assured of your good and honorable intentions," Cooper answered. "Jeremiah!!" He raised his voice, still keeping a firm hold on Montgomery's collar.

"Aye, Jonathan!" The voice answered him from the darkness somewhere beyond the clearing. The woods were alive with sounds now, the noise of the coffle, the slow rumble of the wagon and the impatient, mincing step of many horses.

"The slaves, Hill," Cooper said, careful to keep Montgomery in front of him, "turn them loose."

Montgomery's head jerked sideways as he watched his other men following the line of slaves into the clearing. The two men pulled up short, their eyes on Montgomery, then shifting quickly to Durham and Hill. The bushwhacker nearest Montgomery tensed, his hand going suddenly to his waist. Montgomery struggled against Cooper's grasp and felt the man increase his hold, the front collar of his shirt digging into the flesh at his Adam's apple. "Don't!!" he rasped. "For God's sake, don't!" The bushwhacker nodded tersely, throwing his right hand upwards.

"Bring on the wagon, Jeremiah," Cooper called. He wound his hand tighter in the coarse fabric at Montgomery's neck.

The wagon drove into the clearing, Jeremiah's thick mane of white hair bushing out from beneath his broad-brimmed hat. "It would appear that you have things well in hand, Jonathan," the old man observed. He pulled the team to a halt, winding the lines around the stout hand brake.

"The odds are better now, my friend," Cooper answered. He loosened his hold on Montgomery's collar and addressed the man, a sly sarcasm in his words. "My thanks for bringing them this far North, Montgomery," he said, nodding at the chained blacks, his gaze on the man's profile.

Hill and Durham studied the old man and the wagon, debating their next move. Jeremiah gave a feeble wave of his hand and then pointed a long finger at the pair. "Release them," he ordered, his words soft. When the pair hesitated, he raised his hand and snapped his fingers. One by one, seven armed men stepped out of the shadows, the weapons pointed at the two men. "You'll take no bounty on these poor wretches," Jeremiah intoned. "Not from any man. You'll have your wages," he said, "as agreed but no more."

Hill and Durham exchanged a brief look and then shrugged. Something, they figured, was better than nothing. They dismounted, moving toward Cooper and Montgomery. "He has the keys," Hill said, nodding at Montgomery.

Cooper nodded. "I want your revolvers," he said. He motioned with his own weapon at Hill and Durham first and then at the two men who were still mounted. "Stay on your horses, and drop them on the ground," he ordered. The men did as they were told.

One by one, the Negroes were released. It took a long time and they were sluggish, confused. Gently, Jeremiah waved them towards the wagon, quietly ordering his men to help them up and over the tailgate.

Montgomery watched in silence, his jaws tightly clamped shut, the vein in his neck throbbing. Without turning, he spoke, no longer caring about the pistol that was still pressed into his back. "I'll find you, Cooper;" he promised; "you and all the others." His chest was heaving, rising and falling with each breath he took. The full moon bathed his pale face, taking the color from him. "Mark my words. Unless you kill me, I'll find you."

Cooper shook his head. "There's no need for killing, Montgomery," he said softly. He uncocked his pistol close to the man's ear, and then shoved the weapon back into its holster.

"Maybe there is." The voice came to them from the wagon. A young voice, not as deep as it would someday be.

Cooper inhaled, slowly. "*Runaway*," he whispered.

Montgomery tipped his head slightly as if straining to hear something that threatened to escape him. "Boy?" he whispered. He tensed, like a cat poised at a mouse hole, listening. "Boy!!" he roared.

Runaway dropped down from the wagon, facing the man. "It's been a long time, Elisha," he said.

Montgomery straightened, his eyes sweeping the boy head to toe. "Now," he said. "A hundred years from now, I would have known you!" He advanced a pace, stopping when he saw the pistol the boy held in his hand.

Cooper started across the clearing, following the man.

"Runaway," he called gently. He could see Durham and the others at the corner of his eye; could see them edging toward their horses and their weapons. "Let him go…"

"He killed Charlotte," the boy answered.

Montgomery began to laugh, a vile, scornful sound. "A nigger whore," he said, dragging the words out. His face contorted, a sardonic grin spreading across his moon washed features. He took another step toward the youth. "But you know that, don't you, boy?" he goaded. "That she was a harlot." He laughed again. "Good for a roll in the hay, in the long grass," he took yet another step toward the younger man, pointing at his own crotch. "She used to beg me for this," he said. "For me!"

"Jonathan!?" Jeremiah's voice cut into the silence between Montgomery and the boy, an urgency in him.

Cooper backed up, his gaze darting around the clearing. He felt like man who had struck a match in a strange room only to find out it was filled with a mixture of sulphur and saltpeter. His eyes finally settled on the youth, on the boy's outstretched hand, the pistol.

Runaway had failed to cock the weapon. He stood there, as vulnerable as if he were unarmed.

Montgomery saw the boy's error, too. He could feel Cooper at his back. He kept his eye on the boy, directing his words at the four bushwhackers. "We can take it all," he cajoled. "They're farmers," he pointed at the wagon with the stub of his right arm. "Just farmers! We can take their gold, the niggers. *All* the niggers," he said, swinging the atrophied stub until it pointed directly at Runaway.

Cooper swore under his breath. He could take Montgomery with the first shot, but in the ensuing panic, the aftermath…

A lot of men would die, needlessly. Black and white

alike; they would die. He drew his pistol, cocking the piece
and swinging it in the direction of the four 'slavers. "Get
in the wagon, Runaway," he ordered.

The boy hesitated, a burning deep in his throat. He
kept hearing Montgomery's words over and over. *Nigger
whore. Harlot.*

Montgomery sensed the young man's hesitation, his
confusion. He reached to his belt, fingering the thing that
hung there. "A remembrance, boy," he said softly. He
pulled the long braid free from his waist, tossing it into
the boy's face. *He had learned many things during his
days in Texas.*

Runaway felt the long hair soft against his forehead,
his cheek, and backed away from it. Recoiling, he dropped
his revolver.

And then he realized what it was the man had tossed in
his face. It lay on the ground between them, a scalp lock.
Charlotte's scalp lock. "Oh, God! *God!!*" He screamed
the words and then charged Montgomery, his shoulder
crashing into the man's chest.

Durham moved then, Durham and the other bushwhackers. Cooper threw himself on the ground, firing as he fell.
There was another shot and he fired at the powder flash,
hearing the sound of splintering bone simultaneous with
the impact of the lead bullet. The bushwhackers scattered,
calling to each other as they cursed and struggled with their
panicked animals.

Jeremiah and the others had their hands full with the
frightened blacks. The old man backed the team out of the
clearing, cursing at men and horses alike, his voice roaring
above the wails and confused shouting of the others.

Montgomery was on the ground, the boy pinned beneath him. He was oblivious to the turmoil around them,

the clatter of the horses, the loud clank of the trace irons. Even the explosive shots from the pistols escaped him. There was nothing for him but the boy, just the boy.

He straddled him, one knee on either arm, his good hand wrapped in the thickness of the boy's dark hair. "Texas," he said. He shook the youth's head, sitting down on the boy's chest and moving his knees until Runaway's head was pinned tightly between them. "That's where I learned how to do it," he rasped, releasing his hold on the boy. "From the Mexicans," he dug at his belt, searching for his knife, the words as hurried as his movements. "One swipe, clean as a whistle, and you have a little…" he laughed "…*remembrance*."

Cooper could hear the man's rantings. He rose up out of the dirt, cautiously, cursing the brightness of the moon. Montgomery echoed his curses without realizing it, enraged when he couldn't find his blade. He shook his fist at the heavens and then reached for his revolver. "Your arm first," he threatened. "The right one and then the left." He cocked the revolver, disappointed when the boy didn't cry out, didn't beg.

Moving rapidly, Cooper snake-crawled across the clearing. Less than twenty feet separated him from the boy; from Montgomery. He kept moving, aware that the bushwhackers were still out there, somewhere in the darkness beyond the trees. He rose up on one knee. "*Montgomery!!*" he roared.

Elisha half turned, his revolver still dangerously close to the boy's head. His face was spirit white, translucent beneath the full moon. His features smoothed, a madness lighting his pale eyes. "Ah," he whispered, "the repentant slaver." He lifted his hand, taking aim.

Cooper rose up on both feet. He fired, one shot and two

others answered him, one from Montgomery's pistol and one from the black emptiness rimming the clearing. He felt them both; felt and heard them as they tore into his body. His left leg, just above his knee and then...

... a dull thud in his left side, tearing hot through his belly. He straightened, suspended for a time, his left hand going to his gut. He felt warmth, moist warmth at his fingers, and then he pitched forward.

Montgomery was in the dirt in front of him, the man's eyes staring wide open into the night sky. He was struggling to speak. "Goddamn you," he murmured. He said it out loud then, screaming it into the growing blackness. "Goddamn you!!" They were the last words the man would ever say.

Runaway was on his hands and knees. He crawled forward, reaching out, and his hand hovering above Cooper's head. "Jonathan..." Sobbing, he touched the man's cheek. "Jonathan!!"

Chapter 12

The solitude that had been so much a part of the farm no longer existed. Every day, every night, Runaway relived the agony of what had occurred just outside of Herrin. Even worse were the memories of the long trip home, sitting in the back of the wagon, cradling Cooper's head in his lap, willing the man to live. It had been two months since that terrible journey ended, two long months of fear and worry and guilt.

Cooper was still alive, lying in his own bed, hanging on by some invisible thread that moored him in this world when his body weakened and he began drifting away. Every day they tended to his needs, hoping for some sign of recognition, some sign that he would wake up for more than the few brief moments that were becoming less frequent. He would be lucid then, talking in a whispered hush to Rebecca, at other times summoning Runaway and the girls. Amazingly, through it all, he kept a quick sense of humor, giving in to the melancholy only after a siege of coughing when the pain would come and he would look suddenly old.

Except for his chores, Runaway refused to leave the man's bedside. He slept sitting up in a chair, bolting awake at the slightest sound or change in Cooper's breathing. The youth had been robbed of his childhood, of all family attachments, yet he could not remember experiencing this kind of agony, to genuinely care for someone and to know the sadness of impending loss. In the past, letting go had been such a simple thing, so much so that it meant nothing more than the passing of one day and the beginning of another. But not this time.

Cooper and Runaway were sleeping when Rebecca and the doctor came into the room. The even rise and fall of her husband's soft breathing gave her a temporary sense of peace, a sense of peace she wanted to share with the young man. Gently, she reached out, touching Runaway's shoulder. Her smile was tired but maternal. "Sally needs thee," she murmured. When he tried to protest, she simply shook her head, her voice firm. "The doctor needs to change his bandages and when he's through, I will sit with Jonathan."

Reluctantly, the young man stood up. He waited until she was seated before he left her, pulling the door partially shut. Even then, he hesitated, feeling somehow lost and torn. He could hear Rebecca's soft voice as she began reading from the Scriptures, something comforting — not in the words — but the soft cadence of the woman's voice.

Finally, he released his hold on the doorknob and headed down the hallway. Sally was outside on the front porch. He could hear the quiet back and forth sound of the rocking chair, realizing that there was a sadness in the rhythm he had not noticed before as if the girl was carrying the weight of the world on her fragile shoulders. Without saying anything, he slipped through the door, easing it shut so that he would not startle her.

She was truly great with child now, her belly pressing against the flowered shift she was wearing. Unable to stop himself, Runaway reached out to her, his hand hovering over her misshapen stomach, then dropping to his side. He cared for Sally, loved her for the gentle, forgiving kindness he had found in her, but he could not bring himself to love the thing that was growing within her.

"It's my child, too," she whispered as if she could read his thoughts. Her eyes brimmed with unshed tears and she was trying hard not to cry. She articulated the words carefully, laboring over each one so that she spoke without the plantation dialect Runaway found so offensive. "I've felt it move." She reached out, taking Runaway's hand in her own, pressing it against her stomach. "Rebecca said there is no sin in this child," her eyes were searching Runaway's face, her eyes pleading with him. "I can't hate it, Runaway. No matter how it came to be, I can't hate this chile!" Her growing distress made her careless, the words slurring together.

Unwinding his fingers from the girl's, Runaway backed away. He avoided her eyes, wanting to comfort her but not knowing how. "Jonathan," he said, needing to change the subject. "He could be dying, Sally." He smashed his fist against the porch railing. "He could be dying *and it's my fault!*"

Awkwardly, the girl got to her feet. She moved to his side, reaching out to touch his face. "No," she said softly. "It was Montgomery, Montgomery and the men who were working for him." The girl's face suddenly aged, tiny lines creasing her forehead.

Runaway shook his head. "He called out to Montgomery. They couldn't see him. But he stood up, stood up and called out..." Runaway felt a sore, slow burning deep in his chest. He had to talk about it, get the thing out in the open. "This was going to be his last trip, Sally; the last time he would go so deep into ..." he paused, "... that hell!" He spun the girl around, taking her in his arms and pulling her close, his eyes on the barn. He rested his chin on the girl's soft hair, the tears coming as he remembered his confrontation with Cooper, the night the man had given him his manumission papers. "'*Only thirteen more*'", he whispered, recalling the man's words. He clung to the girl, tighter, drawing strength from her. "It's my fault..." the guilt tore at him.

Sally tensed, her body wracked by a sudden surge of pain that began at the small of her back and then radiated to her swollen belly and down. She cried out, softly, not intending to make any sound, unable to stop herself. "The baby, Runaway..."

He pushed her away, nothing malicious in his move, only gentle concern. There were beads of perspiration on the girl's forehead and a growing puddle of water at her feet. He scooped her up, amazed at how little she weighed, and carried across the porch and toward the front door.

Rebecca was at the stove, a basin of water in her hands. She saw Runaway and the girl and knew at once what was happening. "Elizabeth! Come quickly!" Setting the basin on the table, she opened the door, standing aside. "Put her in thy room, Runaway, and make her as comfortable as thee can." The woman read the worry in the boy's face. "It's going to be all right."

The woman watched after the two, torn between her desire to be with her husband and her desire to help the girl. She turned to her daughter. "Sally's time has come, Elizabeth. She's going to have her baby and she needs the doctor."

The child was stricken. Like the others in the house, she had aged considerably since all the trouble had come to their doorstep. Her gaze shifted to the closed door of her parent's bedroom. "But, Mama, what about Papa?"

Rebecca's eyes closed briefly. She turned back to the woodstove and began ladling fresh water from the reservoir into the basin she had placed on the table. "Thee heard what the doctor said last night, Elizabeth, thee and Naomi. Only God can help Papa now." She picked up the basin and a pile of fresh toweling, carefully handing the supplies to the little girl. "I'm going back to your Papa now. When Jeremiah comes out, thee must take him to Sally. And Elizabeth," she reached out to the child. It was all so unfair, the way life could rob someone this small of something so precious, aging them before their time. "No matter what, thee must do everything Jeremiah tells thee." She stroked the child's head. "Can thee do that for me, Elizabeth?"

The girl's voice was soft, wavering, but she held back the tears. "Yes, Mama."

Rebecca felt the child slip from beneath her fingers. She stood alone for a moment, overwhelmed by the sudden immenseness of a kitchen that had always seemed small, warm and cozy.

This room had been so full, full of life, full of the joy of living, full of the sound of Jonathan's laughter; his deep, resonant voice. She hugged herself, her arms wrapped tightly around her body just below her breasts. She longed for Jonathan's arms, the comfort and secure solace she had always found there in the simplest caress, or (and she felt no shame in this) in the passionate embrace of their late-night couplings. Twenty years, they had been together twenty years and each sunrise had been a new beginning.

The woman roused herself from the rush of sadness

that was sapping her strength. She crossed the room, aware of the sound of her long skirt sweeping the floor as she walked and the hollow sound of her steps; the unnaturally loud snap as she opened the door that led to their bedroom. "Jeremiah," she greeted, forcing a smile.

Jeremiah's head came up slowly, his large grey eyes unfathomable pools of grief. He shook his head, feeling a deep shame at his helplessness. "There's no change, Rebecca." A great sigh escaped the man. "If anything, he's simply slipping farther and farther away."

The woman nodded, her eyes lingering on Jonathan's pale face. "Sally," she said finally. "It's her time." She reached out, smoothing the cover at Jonathan's chin. She could feel Naomi watching her from the high-backed rocker in the corner; the little girl perched on the edge of the seat, her feet not quite reaching the floor. Rebecca inhaled deeply, forcing yet another smile, this one for the little girl. "There is a trunk in the attic, Naomi, the one with the rainbow quilt on it." She kept her voice light, opening her arms as the child ran to her. "It's full of all sort of treasures," she reached down, cupping the child's chin in her palm, her fingers stroking the girl's cheek. "All thy clothes, from when thee and Elizabeth were first born. Sally will need them," she intoned, "Sally and the new baby."

Naomi clung to her mother's skirt for a time. She was a different child than Elizabeth. Naomi needed a secret place away from the pain, a private place where she could hide and pretend that nothing in her world had changed. She pulled away from her mother and fled the room without looking back to the place where her father lay.

"Jeremiah," Rebecca called out to the physician again. "Sally needs thee."

The old man began fussing with the black satchel on

the nightstand beside the bed. He looked even older than his sixty-five years. Shaking his head, he closed his bag, staring down at the man lying on the bed. *It was such a waste*, he observed. Jonathan was a good man, a decent man who had labored hard to make amends for the sins of his youth. Jeremiah picked up his satchel, crossing the room to where Rebecca stood. He reached out, his fingers gently touching her elbow. "I'm sorry, Rebecca," he said. It was more than grief. He was apologizing for his failure as a physician.

Rebecca understood the man's words. She faced him, reading the agony behind the pale eyes. "Thee brought him home to me, Jeremiah." She closed her eyes briefly, imagining the horror of that long ride, the way the old man must have fought to keep Jonathan alive. "Thee brought him home and I will always be grateful for that."

Jeremiah pulled himself erect, fighting the fatigue that tore at him, finding comfort in the woman's words. "I'll see to the girl," he promised.

Rebecca was alone now, alone with Jonathan. She went to the other side of the bed, the side where she normally slept. Gently, she eased down onto the heavy quilts, as if she were simply going to bed.

There was an antiseptic smell to the room, to everything in the room. Camphor and eucalyptus to ease Jonathan's labored breathing and the pungent smell of the ointments and powders Jeremiah had used to dress Jonathan's words. No more the light fragrance of her perfume, the sweet scent Jonathan loved so much, and Rebecca's one worldly vanity, the lavender cologne that Jonathan always bought her at Christmas, one of the few compromises made regarding her Quaker faith but a holiday Jonathan enjoyed and wanted to share with his wife and children.

Lavender. Always lavender, in tiny, intricately turned crystal vials etched with scenes from the countries of their origin. Her dresser was full of them, and the windowsill above their bed. The sun shone through them, the triangular projections on the glass stoppers acting like a prism, cutting and diffusing the light into a myriad of rainbows that spilled across their blankets and the white pine floor.

The woman reached out, her hand warm on the man's forehead. He was cold, so very cold. That first night, when Runaway and Jeremiah had carried him into the room he had burned with fever. They had tied him to the bed, quieting his loud ranting as he seemed to melt like a child's wax doll.

He had relived so much in those long, feverish days and nights, the torments that he had hidden away in the locked closet of his mind, the guilt. Runaway and Rebecca had stood beside the bed, listening to him as he begged people long dead for their forgiveness.

And then the fever had broken, and he was awake, awake and aware for just a small moment in the early hours before dawn. Rebecca was with him and Elizabeth had appeared at her side like some miniature wraith, summoned somehow from her sleep by a need that Rebecca could neither understand nor comprehend. It was as if the child somehow knew her father was awake. *I love you, Papa*, she had breathed, her small hands swallowed up by one of his. She kissed him then and left the room to fetch Naomi and Runaway.

Jonathan had slipped back into the deep sleep that so often precedes death before Runaway and the girls came back. He lay still and white against the pillows, as if napping, his breathing shallow but regular, and for weeks that was how he remained.

Except for the few times when he would miraculously become aware, those brief times when he would speak to them and they could all pretend he was getting better.

Rebecca leaned forward, her lips brushing the man's cold cheek. Even his breath had a chill to it now as it whispered past her ear. She clung to him, wishing that she could give him some of her warmth and felt the hot sting of a single tear as it rolled down her cheek. "I love thee, Jonathan Thomas Cooper. Dear God, *how I have always loved thee.*"

The man sighed or that's how it seemed, as if a great, heavy burden had been taken from his shoulders. Rebecca lifted herself away from him, her fingers tracing the smooth forehead, the sandy-colored eyebrows, his lips. She kissed him then, knowing it was for the last time.

And as one life whispered to an end in this room — in the bedroom at the front of the house — another life struggled to make a new beginning.

***

Sally screamed, a long, pain-filled scream that seemed to originate from the tortured opening between her legs. It was as if great hands were tearing at her, forcing her thighs wide apart, the very bones feeling as though they were being torn from her hip sockets.

"Help her!" Runaway grabbed the girl's hands, pressing them prayer-like across her breasts, holding her. "Please, Jeremiah! *Help her!!*" He was begging the man.

Jeremiah straightened, his face mottled, angry. He grabbed the towel Elizabeth had brought him and wiped his hands. "I'll need Rebecca," he said. He strode from the room, picking up Elizabeth as he hurried through the door. Rebecca had just stepped into the hallway leading to the kitchen, her hand still on the porcelain doorknob. She could see the worry in Jeremiah's face and the terror in her daughter's. She pulled the door shut. "Naomi is in the attic, Elizabeth. Go to her." She turned her eyes back to the old man, watching as he gathered stacks of toweling in his arms. "Does thee need me, Jeremiah?"

The old man looked at the woman, at her drawn features. He nodded without speaking, his eyes drifting to the closed bedroom door. He knew without asking that Jonathan was dead. "Breech," the word came like a curse. "The child is coming breech." Behind him, Sally screamed again and he turned, beckoning for the woman to follow him. "Children begetting children," he said, hurrying into the room. He rolled up his sleeves, extending his arms, watching as Rebecca poured the remainder of a bottle of his medicinal brandy over his exposed hands. "It's sinful," he snorted, "a man doing this to a child!"

He returned to the bed, his hands disappearing beneath the sheeting that covered Sally's belly. The girl was panting, her fingers laced around Runaway's forearm, the nails biting into the hard muscle above the boy's wrists. "Hurt," she breathed, her face contorted as another contraction tore at her. She screamed again, unable to stop herself and when the scream died there was the slippery sound of flesh tearing.

"Don't cry, child," Jeremiah coaxed, his hand pressing on her abdomen. Each sob halted the contractions, worked against them. "She's too small," the old man breathed, "too damned small!!"

Rebecca was at the man's shoulder. She could see a tiny buttock exposed, a tiny buttock and part of a miniature foot. The girl had dilated well beyond the norm, the opening of the birth canal forced even wider by the unnatural position of the infant. There was another hard contraction and the sound of more tearing, the girl stifling a scream as she tried to scoot away from the pain. Sally tried to draw her knees up to her chest and was stopped by a sharp command from Jeremiah. "Work with it, girl!" he ordered. "When the pain comes, push!"

Using two fingers, Jeremiah penetrated the girl's vaginal opening, making a slow, purposeful circle, his free hand on Sally's knee. He exchanged a long look with Runaway, using his fingers as invisible eyes as he probed at the unborn infant. "The other foot," he said, more to himself than the others. Waiting until the contraction passed, he manipulated the tiny body, gently pushing the baby back into the birth canal. "If I can free the other foot." He disappeared beneath the sheeting that now concealed the girl's knees, his fingers busy, and one hand on her belly. The next contraction was starting, he could feel the uterus bunching beneath his palm and knew there was little time.

The room was quiet, unnaturally quiet. Runaway stood at Sally's head, his eyes on the growing smear of blood on the sheet beneath her spread legs. He swallowed, feeling sick, his stomach churning. Sally's grip had eased and he stroked her hand, feeling the sweat.

They waited, the only sound the girl's labored breathing and the uneven, slow drag of the pendulum on the Thomas clock on the dresser. *Tick-tock, tick-tock,* and then the slow grind as the mechanism poised to strike the quarter-hour. The large hand jumped, triggering the chime and Runaway felt the girl's hand tense again.

"Now," Jeremiah whispered. The contraction came, a strong one and he pressed down firmly on the girl's stomach. Hidden from view, two tiny feet were clenched in the fingers of his other hand.

There was no outcry from the girl this time, just a low guttural moan — a grunting — as if she were laboring to pick up a heavy burden. She strained against the tugging she felt between her legs, untangling her fingers from Runaway and pressing them against her belly, just below her breasts. There was a strange, not totally uncomfortable feeling at her crotch, a slippery wiggling as the child slid from within her.

There was no sound, no cries. Sally lifted her head, struggling to sit up, resting on her elbows as a wave of nausea swept her. The room was spinning, the bed seeming to bob up and down like a small, open boat being pitched about on a storm-tossed sea.

Jeremiah and Rebecca were busy at the foot of the bed, their movements hurried. And then Jeremiah held the child up by its feet, smacking the tiny rump with three fingers. Once, twice, a third time.

There was a weak, sputtery cough. Wet, like a child with a chest cold trying to clear congested lungs, then another cough, and another. And then rage, the strong, gusty cry of rage as if birth were an insult and entrance into this new world was something to despise.

Rebecca reached out, her hand on Sally's knee. "A girl," she smiled. "Thee has a beautiful, baby girl."

Sally eased back onto the pillows, her arms outstretched as she waited for Jeremiah to finish his inspection. Then the child was in her arms and she was oblivious to Jeremiah's continued medical attention, the baby warm against her breast. "Look at her, Runaway," she smiled, folding back the swaddling cloth. "*Look at her.*"

Runaway hesitated, haunted by a flood of memories that just as quickly faded. He shook them away, reaching out to finger the small flannel blanket. The child was a mass of wrinkles, her small head covered with a thick blanket of moist, dark hair. Runaway touched her head, winding a single curl around his forefinger. Her hair was soft, so very soft. He studied the child more closely. She was a miniature Sally, the same complexion, the same long fingers and tiny, fragile frame. "She is beautiful, Sally," he breathed, awed by the wonder of something so small, yet so...

...*strong*. Runaway had witnessed the way the child had fought to take its first breath, the way it scrunched up its eyes at the light that had intruded into its world. He had sensed the anger in her as she shook her fists in outrage at Jeremiah's probing touch as if she blamed the old man for taking her from a place where she had been safe.

Rebecca touched Runaway's shoulder. "Thee has just seen a miracle," she said softly.

Runaway nodded. He faced the woman. "Jonathan?" he asked.

Rebecca bit her bottom lip, not wanting to answer. "Jonathan is dead, Runaway," she whispered. And then, needing to be alone, she left the room and retreated to the place she most wanted to be, with Jonathan and twenty years of memories she could not bear — for now — to share.

***

The summer had been long and hot, and there had been little rain. Concern about the war took a back seat to the very real fear over crops that withered beneath an unrelenting August sun. Runaway worked long hours in the fields, supervising the young boys Rebecca had hired to help with the endless chores. Together, they built a series of channels, irrigation canals similar to the ones Runaway remembered from the time he had spent on a farm where the owner had decided to grow rice. The technology was crude, drawing water from the two small rivers that bordered the farm but the corn crop and the alfalfa were saved.

Rebecca, Sally and the girls had modified Runaway's system, using water from the family well and a series of miniature waterwheels to periodically flood the family garden. It was more play than work for the twins, the little girls splashing barefoot and ankle deep in the little channels, their rare laughter a welcome sound in a place where grief had been so prevalent.

Elizabeth was playing in the mud now, dressed in a sleeveless cotton shift and covered head to toe in the rich, black silt. Naomi stood beside her, satisfied to watch, more restrained in her play, carefully rinsing her own feet and lifting her long skirt in an attempt to stay clean. Rebecca stood on the porch, watching them. She didn't have the heart to stop their play, secretly wishing she was a child again and free to join them. This is how she wanted them to stay, innocent and ignorant of the cruelty in the world beyond this place, the same cruelty that had robbed them of their father and their brother.

"Rebecca?" Runaway reached out, touching the woman's shoulder.

She turned to face the young man, surprised when she saw that he was holding a glass of lemonade. "You found ice," she smiled, taking the glass. Instead of drinking it, she raised the cold glass to her face and pressed it against her forehead.

Runaway was sucking on a piece of the ice that had been in the bottom of his glass. He pushed it to the side of his mouth so that he could speak. "Two small cakes left beneath the final layer of straw," he said. He and Jeremiah and a crew from Rebecca's congregation had sawed the blocks of ice from the river when Jonathan was still alive, storing them in the ice shed behind the stock barns. He remembered chipping away at the ice, bringing it into the house to ease the fevers that had tormented the older man and closed his eyes against the memories. "I'm going to have to dunk Elizabeth in the river before she can come in the house," he said finally, pointing at the little girls.

Rebecca was sipping her lemonade, enjoying the tart sweetness as much as the cold. The year that had started with such promise was more than half over, 1863, a New Year and what should have been a new beginning, she thought. And then Jonathan...

Emancipation was now the law, but the War still continued with great losses for both North and South. Fugitive slaves were still coming to the farm for temporary refuge but not so many as before and the danger of helping them had increased. Yet she could not turn them away. That much she owed Jonathan's memory, as well as her own growing beliefs, that — in spite of the spirited ramblings of the Southern zealots — there was no such thing as a *Holy War* and no man or woman had the right to deny another freedom.

"Mama?" Elizabeth was on the porch, standing in front of her mother. A wet path led from the garden's edge, in line with the damp footprints, to the front steps and upwards to where the child was standing.

"Elizabeth." Unable to hide the laughter, Rebecca bent down, her hands hovering above the child's shoulders.

"Look, Mama," the little girl whispered. She reached out, her fingers closing around Runaway's right hand. The mud that was beginning to dry on her arms had taken on a mahogany hue, a thin patina forming. "We're the same, Mama!"

It was true. The pale brown veneer on the child's arm matched the natural hue of the young man's skin. Rebecca considered her daughter's words, aware of the silence behind and to the right of her shoulder. Using one finger, she wiped off a small measure of mud, exposing her daughter's fair skin. "That," she said softly, flaking the soil away, "and this," she tapped the girl's lighter flesh, "are shells, Elizabeth, like the shells on the eggs thee brings me every morning. Eggs with brown shells, eggs with white shells." She was quiet a moment, considering her next words. "What happens to the shells, Elizabeth?"

The child's brow furrowed, a small frown tugging at the corners of her mouth. "We throw them away," she said finally.

Rebecca was nodding. "It's what thee finds *inside* a thing that is important, not what covers it." Her left hand was on Runaway's arm now and she squeezed it slightly. At the same time, she was gently thumping her daughter's chest with the index finger of her right hand.

Elizabeth's face brightened, her blue eyes lighting with a sudden awareness. "A good heart!" she said suddenly.

Rebecca straightened. "Yes," she said, content and proud that her daughter understood. "Thee are like Runaway because thee has a very good heart!"

Runaway reached down, scooping the little girl up in his arms. "A good heart, but dirty feet," he scolded. "But I know how to fix that!" Laughing, he sprinted down the stairs and across the yard, heading for the clear water at the edge of the river. Naomi fell in behind, both girls shrieking in joy as Runaway plunged into the water.

***

Jonathan's birthday had come and gone, marked by an awkward evening meal that was somehow more ceremony than celebration. The twins had insisted on some kind of remembrance and then fled the table in tears when the conversation faded to a hollow nothingness. It affected everyone. Even Sally's baby — the child she had named Charlotte in the hope Runaway would learn to love her — had been exceedingly cranky. Only Rebecca remained strong, cleaning up a table full of food that had been barely touched; boxing the leftovers and driving miles to deliver a feast to a family of fugitives Jeremiah had taken in on their run north.

Runaway had withdrawn to the fields and to the mundane chores that kept him away from the house. He was at the woodpile now, chopping kindling. He worked at the wood with a small hand ax, whittling away at the larger pieces with no real purpose. There was plenty of kindling in the wood box in the kitchen and a larger pile beside the outer kitchen door.

"Thee are working too hard, Runaway." Rebecca had come up behind the youth, a flannel cloak thrown over her shoulders. She held it in place with one hand, her eyes on the hills north of the house. The trees were losing their color, the leaves turning pale brown and becoming brittle. Soon the branches would be bare, dark fingers against a grey sky.

"There's a lot of work to be done before winter," the young man answered. He kept on with his chopping, quartering yet another small log.

Rebecca reached out, her hand firm on the boy's forearm, restraining him. "Come to the house, Runaway." She was not asking this time. "Thee and I must talk."

The youth stopped in his chore, smashing the axe into

the huge stump he had been using as a chopping block. "Rebecca..." He turned, facing the woman. "Please, Rebecca."

The woman shook her head, her concern drawing tiny lines around her eyes, her mouth. "It's not right, Runaway, to set yourself apart or to be so alone in a house full of people." She took the boy's arm, leading him across the farmyard to the house.

The kitchen was warm and yet Runaway took no comfort from it. He took Rebecca's cloak and hung it on the row of pegs beside the door and then removed his own coat. Rebecca was already at the stove, brewing a pot of strong tea. She poured them both a cup, carrying them to the table, nodding at the young man's chair.

Runaway sat, unable to face the woman. He helped himself to a spoonful of strained honey, stirring it into the steaming cup of tea. "It's so quiet," he said, making empty conversation.

"Sally has the children with her in the parlor." She pointed to the closed draperies, her voice soft. "She gave me these," she said, taking a small stack of thumb worn pamphlets from her apron pocket, "this morning." She rippled the pages with a crooked forefinger.

"She had no right!" Runaway reached out, taking the booklets. He held them for a time and then flung them across the room.

"Mr. Outerbridge sent them to you," Rebecca said, ignoring the young man's show of temper.

Runaway shoved his full cup away and stood up, his hands knotted around the back of his chair. He stared across the table to the seat at the head of the table. *Jonathan's place. Because of his stubbornness and his stupidity, Jonathan was dead, and his place at the head of the table was empty, would always be empty.* "They're nothing," he said, shifting his gaze to the scattered pages. "*Nothing!*"

Rebecca sipped her tea, her eyes on the young man. She put the cup back down on the table, both hands wrapped around the warmth of the mug. "I would not call the writings of a man like Frederick Douglass or a woman like Harriet Jacobs nothing." She took another drink of the tea. "Douglass is a great man, Runaway." She faced the youth again, her right eyebrow arched. "I heard him speak once at an Abolitionists' Meeting. And Jonathan and I both read the *North Star*." She brightened. "He campaigned for President Lincoln, Runaway. Thee should have heard him..."

Runaway shoved his chair back into place, hard. He couldn't understand Rebecca, the way she went on day by day as if nothing had really happened. Cooking. Tending the girls. Reading to them, teaching them. Laughing with them. *As if Jonathan hadn't died, as if he were away on a trip and they were simply waiting for him to come back.* "Don't you miss him!?" he asked, the words as harsh as if he had shouted them. "*Don't you hate it that he'll never come back?*" Immediately, he regretted his outburst, his agony more intense when he realized he could never take the words back or properly apologize for them.

Rebecca considered the boy's question, her eyes on the far wall. "I was seventeen when I married him," she said finally, a smile pulling at the corners of her mouth. "And Jonathan..." she paused, her eyes narrowing as if she was seeing it all again. "Jonathan was just twenty-one." She inhaled and the smile grew. "Boston," she said. "I was in Boston, visiting my aunt. Out of school, just back from a grand tour of Europe, my Grandmother had insisted I take. I thought I was so wise." She laughed then, a quiet, joyful laugh. "He cut such a fine figure in his master's uniform. And he was such a flirt!" She stopped, enjoying for a moment some secret memory that warmed her. "He thought every woman in Boston was in love with him!" The woman shook her head and then faced Runaway. "I let him chase me right up until I caught him," she finished. She was quiet then, reflective. "Yes, I miss him, Runaway," she said, her mood changing. She visibly aged before the boy, tired lines forming at her mouth and forehead. "The mornings are the hardest, when I wake up and reach out to touch him…" Her voice broke then, and she took a large swallow of tea. "Jonathan would not want me to grieve for him forever," she said, her finger tracing the rim of the cup. "To love him, to encourage the girls to love and remember him — these things he would want. But to spend my life," she lifted her head, her eyes boring into the youth, "being sorry for things I did or did not do, or could have done differently…?" She shook her head. "That's not grief, Runaway," she said, castigating the boy with her words, her look, "that's guilt.

"Thee are not grieving for Jonathan, Runaway." It was perhaps the first time she truly saw what had been driving the young man. "Thee are too filled with guilt to grieve for Jonathan."

Stunned, Runaway sat down in his chair. "I…" he couldn't find the words. "I…"

Rebecca reached out, pressing her fingers against his lips. "Thee sulks around the farm, not speaking to anyone. Not Sally, not the girls. At times, not even me. Thee buries thyself in thy work…"

Runaway took the woman's hands. "I *owe* you, Rebecca. *I owe Jonathan*." It *was* guilt, and it was tearing at him as viciously as a crow on carrion.

"No," the woman said. "Thee owes nothing."

"But it's my fault, my fault that Jonathan isn't here!" It was out, finally spoken after all the long weeks and months, the great cancer that had been eating at him. "I do the work that Jonathan would have done. *It's my job to do the work Jonathan would have done!*"

Rebecca shook her head. "Thee has exchanged one form of slavery for another with no hope of ever being free." She patted his arm. "Jonathan would not want thee to live like this.

"He did not die for thee to live like this."

Runaway felt a heaviness in his chest that threatened to suffocate him. His head throbbed and his eyes burned and he swore. "*Damn!*" He was being weak, so damned weak. *'Jonathan would not want thee to live like this.'* He heard the woman's words again, finally understanding their meaning. The tears came then, a flood of tears.

Rebecca held him, her fingers stroking his aching temples. She had shed her tears. In the long, empty nights after they had put Jonathan in the ground on the small rise above the house among the dormant apple trees, next to their son. She had shed her tears until there were none left and death finally released its hold on her soul.

Chapter 13

The recruiting station at Herrin was nothing more than a canvas tent hastily erected in a vacant lot between the general store and the post office. The remnants of burned rubble littered the ground at the entrance, the charred remains of a jewelry store that had been targeted and destroyed during a nighttime raid by southern sympathizers. The Union military had been quick to respond to the owner's request for help, the man had lost three sons the previous summer at the Battle of Gettysburg.

Martial law had been declared and a temporary curfew imposed while order was restored. Afterwards, it had been the decision of a young major from Baltimore to plant a Union flag on the spot where the Copperheads had vented their hatred. His next step was to turn the place into a recruiting office actively seeking the enlistment of both freed and fugitive Negroes.

A company of like-minded and seasoned veterans was more than happy to assure that the young officer's orders were fully carried out and dignity maintained. They patrolled the streets in pairs, smartly dressed in their new winter issue, grateful for the brief respite from the fighting. It was, they knew, a temporary posting, something they chose not to share with the locals. The winds of war favored the North for now but those winds could change just as the loyalties of the people in this small prairie town could change.

Runaway was standing shoulder-to-shoulder with Jeremiah, both of them carefully observing the activity in the street. It was something new for the younger man. Rebecca had insisted he be "properly" dressed and he was wearing clothing more suited for a gentleman farmer than a former slave.

Jeremiah poked him in the ribs, something playful in the old man's mood. "Feeling uppity?" he whispered, enjoying the way the younger man seemed to be dancing in place.

The smile was slow in coming, but it was genuine. "No," Runaway answered finally. He had learned much about the old doctor in the past months. Jeremiah was someone Rebecca referred to as a true, Christian gentleman. A physician by training, Jeremiah also had a degree in divinity and another in horticulture. He was outspoken in his beliefs, stubborn in his determination to heal the body and downright hateful to anyone who toyed with the harmony he saw in nature. And above all, he felt that War was an abomination.

And yet he had brought Runaway to this place knowing full well what the young man intended.

Jeremiah poked him again, his voice soft. "I think you're next, boy," he said gently.

Runaway had not realized that the line he had been standing in had progressed this far up the boardwalk. "Jeremiah …"

The young major had chosen this particular time to

join the sergeant at the cluttered table. His smile was somehow bemused as if he was wondering which of the two men standing before him he should speak to first. Humor, he decided, would be the best approach. "Am I to assume, sir," he began, addressing Jeremiah, "you have come to enlist?"

Jeremiah's laughter came from deep within, booming into the silence of the small tent and resonating to the street beyond. "Are you in need of someone to take over your job, son?"

It was the officer's turn to laugh. "Major Quinton, sir," he greeted, extending his hand. "I think you're more General material."

"Dr. Jeremiah Hawkings," he shook the younger man's hand at the same time giving him a quick once over. He reckoned the soldier's age to be thirty or so and knew from the wedding ring on his left hand — a gold band still shiny from its newness — that it hadn't been that long since the man had left hearth and home and, probably, some desk in Washington. Still, he had the sense of command about him, and a quiet wisdom far beyond his years. Dark eyes and hair and a meticulously groomed mustache and goatee set well in a face that was attractive in a classical sense and somehow familiar. "Booth," Jeremiah whispered, "Edwin Booth!" The resemblance was uncanny.

Again, the officer laughed. "I consider it a curse looking like some dandy who makes his living reciting what someone else has written! But the ladies…" His cheeks flushed.

Jeremiah could feel Runaway growing restless beside him. It was a good time to discuss the business at hand. "And this young man, Major?" he asked, encouraging Runaway to step forward. "What kind of job can you offer this young man?"

Quinton's eyes narrowed. He pulled himself to his full height, something a shade under 5' 10 and was surprised to find that he was somewhat shorter than the young man that stood before him. "Can he speak for himself?"

Runaway returned the man's scrutiny. Months of being tutored by both Jeremiah and Rebecca in manners as well as more scholarly pursuits had taught him — finally — to consider his answers before he blurted them out. Still, it was a struggle. "Yes, sir, I can speak for myself." The smile didn't quite reach his eyes. "I'm here to enlist."

Quinton nodded. The older man no longer interested him. "As a freedman?" It was a question he hated asking but a necessity. Fugitive slaves required particularly delicate handling, especially in a place where southern sympathizers could and did cause problems. That's why he had been appointed to this current endeavor. A third-generation abolitionist, Roman Quinton was extremely clever when it came to protecting fugitive blacks.

Runaway reached into his inside jacket pocket. "As a free man," he answered. He opened the leather wallet, something ceremonial in the way he withdrew the papers and placed them on the man's makeshift desk.

It was the first time since before Jonathan's death Jeremiah had seen the documents. He stood, peering over the younger man's shoulder, reading the upside-down words with ease. There was a sudden rush of air as he inhaled sharply, the surprise evident.

Startled, Quinton looked up. "Is there something wrong, Dr. Hawkings?"

Ashamed that he had failed to maintain his usual control, Jeremiah was almost contrite. "No," he answered finally. Then, knowing that more was needed, he continued. His hand was on Runaway's shoulder when he finally spoke. "I've known this young man for quite some time," he said softly. "When he first came to us, he had no proper name, not in the sense that you and I have a name." He reached out a long finger, tapping it against the topmost paper. "Thomas Cooper." There was a genuine reverence in the words when the old man said them. "He has chosen the family name of a good friend and a fine man."

Quinton's gaze had shifted again to Runaway. He was more successful than Jeremiah at hiding his emotions and the fact that he recognized the Cooper name. Jonathan Cooper had become a martyr to the cause of the northern Abolitionists, a redeemed sinner who had been willing to sacrifice his life for those he had harmed so grievously in the past. "He gave you your freedom?" he asked, the words precise and loud enough that those just outside the tent could hear them.

The younger man stood erect and proud. "He gave me a new life," he answered.

An awkward silence prevailed for a time, interrupted by the shuffling of feet on the boardwalk behind them. All three men shared a moment of nervous laughter before Quinton found his voice. "Can you make you mark?" he asked. Hurriedly, he pulled a sheaf of papers from the thick portfolio that lay between them.

At another time, in another place, the question would have provoked an angry response from the younger man. This time, however, Runaway did not feel offended. He took the papers, quickly reading them. Then, as naturally as if he had been doing it every day of his life, he signed — for the first time — the name he had chosen, the name Rebecca and the girls had so freely given, Thomas Cooper.

Quinton picked up the final sheet. There, in eloquent and flawless Spenserian script was the young man's signature. "And how are you at mathematics, Private Cooper? Please tell me you are proficient in mathematics."

***

Jeremiah had arranged supper at the home of a fellow clergyman, a place where he and Runaway could eat at the same table without the usual problem of forced segregation. They were alone now, lingering over coffee and dessert. "Do you understand, Runa …" he paused, correcting himself, "Thomas, what my true feelings are about what you are doing?"

The younger man was toying with a piece of pumpkin pie, wishing it tasted the same as the pies Rebecca had taught Sally to bake. It puzzled him, the complexity of Jeremiah's mind. "I don't understand," he breathed shaking his head; "any of it." He changed the subject, ignoring the man's original question, still nervous about the fact Jeremiah had chosen Herrin as the place he would enlist. The little town was just fifty miles east of Missouri on one side, and less than that from Kentucky and the southern-most point of Indiana on the other. *It was like jumping from the frying pan into the fire,* he mused.

Almost as if he could read the younger man's mind, Jeremiah spoke. "I chose Herrin for a reason, Thomas," he said softly. "The railroad is moving freight again," he smiled. He was gazing at the window on the far wall, welcoming the growing darkness. "If I'm *here*" he stressed the word, "if *we* are here where people can see us, we can't be transporting any fugitives." The old man took a long drink from his mug, the smile still there when he set down the empty cup.

The younger man was unable to conceal his surprise. "Rebecca said nothing…" his voice trailed off, and he was suddenly filled with a nagging concern.

Jeremiah was shaking his head. "Rebecca knows nothing about the people who are coming this time," he said. "They will bypass the farm." He inhaled. "It was never Jonathan's intention to put Rebecca and the children at risk. He did his work far away from the place where he lived in order to keep them safe. We need to make things right again, Thomas. We need to put Rebecca and the children out of harm's way, especially now."

The young man shoved his plate away and stood up. "Are you telling me I shouldn't have done this?" he gestured at the uniform he was now wearing. A mixture of guilt and panic tore at him. Nervously, he smoothed his hair, running his fingers through the close-cropped curls that he had trimmed that very morning.

"I asked you in the beginning of this conversation," Jeremiah's voice carried a gentle censure, "if you understood my feelings about what you were doing." He raised his hand when the other started to speak, silencing him. "Every man has choices to make throughout his life," he continued. "Some good, some bad, some moral, some …" he shrugged. "I know that you need to do this thing, Thomas. In spite of what I feel — what Rebecca feels — about the insanity of war, *any* war. Brother against brother …" the disgust was evident in his voice; his anger growing. He inhaled, forcing a calmness he didn't feel. "I've been to the field hospitals, I've seen the carnage! All the fine young men, in the prime of their lives …"

There was a deep need in Thomas to vindicate the choices he had made. "The Bible," he whispered. "… '*In the spring, when Kings go to war…*'"he was paraphrasing the words he had read throughout the Old Testament. "Saul. David. All the kings."

Jeremiah slammed his clenched fist against the table, so hard that the china and silverware clattered against the heavy oak. "Words!" he roared. "Divinely inspired to be sure, but not so divinely transcribed!!" He was on his feet now, facing the younger man.

The silence between the two men was intense, more intense than the sudden explosion of words. Jeremiah was the first to speak. He reached out, gently placing his right hand on the other's left shoulder, turning the gesture to a gentle pat. "Consider the heart of the message, Thomas, and let that guide you in the future."

Perplexed, Thomas watched as the older man withdrew. He knew their conversation was over and was — he realized — grateful that it had ended. There was so much he did not understand, so much he needed to learn. '*Consider the heart of the message…*'

Chapter 14

November arrived with a vengeance, on the heels of a late Indian summer that had turned deadly cold almost without warning. A thin dusting of snow came, barely two inches, followed by a sleet storm that left a glassy frosting across the prairie landscape. Rebecca stood at the kitchen window, watching as a cotton-tail rabbit skittered across the icy turf, something comic in the way the animal would attempt to hop forward up the small hill, only to slide back down to the bottom. She smiled, hearing the squirrels in the eaves chattering as if they were cheering the rabbit on, or — perhaps — mocking its efforts.

"Rebecca?" Sally joined her at the window. She was holding her baby, balancing the child on one hip. "Is someone coming?" It had been a long time since there had been any company and she was hopeful.

The entire house was waking up now. Rebecca could hear the girls whispering in their bedroom and then the soft patter of stockinged feet as they trotted down the hallway. They were still in their flannel nightshirts, wrapped in the small quilts Sally and Rebecca had pieced together just weeks before. Both of them headed for the kitchen stove, seeking the warmth radiating from the cast iron, careful not to get too close.

It was then that they heard the sounds. Muted at first, just a small whisper above the wind then growing. Elizabeth was the first to speak. "Mama?" She dropped her quilt and moved quickly across the floor to stand at her mother's side. The child had not been motivated by fear but out of concern and it was clear that her intention was to help if needed.

Rebecca moved closer to the front window. She had picked up a metal spatula from the dry sink and she used it now to scrape the thin layer of hoarfrost that had formed on the glass. The noise was still being carried by the wind but there was nothing to be seen on the horizon or beyond the curve in the road leading to the farmhouse.

And then she heard the voices and the cadenced singing: *"...the Hebrew children from the fiery furnace, then why not every man?"*

The next sound was the precise step of marching feet, mixed with the soft jingle of saddle tack and the plodding of shod hooves. Rebecca watched as they finally came into view. The troopers marched four abreast in a column twelve deep. Two men leading horses — one white, one a Negro — marched beside them.

Elizabeth was on her tiptoes at the window, the first to fully see. "Thomas!! Mama, Sally! It's Thomas!"

***

Major Quinton was sitting at the kitchen table, using the cup of coffee as a hand warmer. It had been a long time since he had enjoyed something that didn't have the bitter tang of chicory and he was determined to make it last. He also was glad to be out of the wind and to know that his men were also bivouacked in a shelter with four walls and a roof. "I really am sorry for the imposition, Mrs. Cooper," he began, feeling the need to apologize to the woman. "But ever so grateful for the shelter!"

Rebecca was busy at the sink, supervising the coming and going of the young black woman and the twin girls. "Thee brought Thomas home to us, Major Quinton. That is no imposition! And there is more than enough room in the barn for your soldiers." The warmth in the woman's voice was genuine, as was her smile. Her smile broadened when Thomas stomped through the door and she watched him shake off the snow.

Thomas returned the woman's silent greeting with a smile of his own but his words were directed at the Major. "The men are quartered, sir, and the stock tended."

Quinton nodded. He took a long drink from his cup before speaking. When he did, the formality was gone from his voice and his words. "I think, Sergeant, we can dispense with the formalities for a time. This is your home and I'm your guest. Can you handle that?"

Rebecca interrupted before Thomas had a chance to speak. "I think, Mr. Quinton, it would be a fine thing. I also think it would save a lot of standing up, saluting, coming to attention…" She stopped, embarrassed that she had spoken out so brazenly. But she was not about to apologize.

Quinton was smiling when he stood up. He bowed and held out his cup. "My mother would have my head if I didn't stand up when greeting a lady or when asking for a second cup of coffee. Would you have me abandon good manners as well?"

Rebecca laughed, something good-natured in the sound.

"I think I would like to meet thy mother, Mr. Quinton." Then, just as quickly, she turned from the man, her attention on the task at hand. "Thomas, we'll need some things from the smoke house." Her eyes narrowed as she did some quick mental ciphering. "Also from the cellar." The enormity of the job she was anticipating suddenly struck her. "Dishes," she sighed.

Quinton was on his feet again. "Is there anything I can do?" He didn't understand yet what she was intending.

Rebecca nodded and began issuing orders. "We'll need three hams, Thomas, and at least a peck of potatoes." She inhaled. "Molasses, some brown sugar. Dried apples." She began moving about the kitchen again, quietly instructing the girls and Sally.

"Major," Thomas reached out, touching the other man's arm. "I'll need help with the meat and the other provisions." He grabbed his own coat from the hook beside the door and waited for the man to join him.

It was then the Major realized what the woman intended on doing. "She means to feed us all!"

Thomas laughed. "She *will* feed us all."

Before they had even made through the door, Rebecca called to them again. "Thomas! We'll need the large copper boiler and you'll have to start up the woodstove in the summer kitchen!"

Without meaning to, both men saluted and then beat a hasty retreat.

***

By seven o'clock that evening, the troopers in Major Quinton's command had been fed in grand style. Through some magic the young Major didn't completely comprehend,

Rebecca, Sally and the two little girls (with minimal help from Thomas and himself) had managed to serve hot ham, mashed potatoes, white gravy, sweet potatoes and fried apples for fifty men. The copper boiler had been filled with sweet cider and cinnamon sticks for those who didn't crave coffee or tea and not one man in the barn could complain of an empty stomach or a dry throat.

Quinton had "pulled rank" when it came time to clean up. Handpicking six of the troopers he knew well, he detailed the men to kitchen duty and insisted that Rebecca, Sally and the girls retire to the parlor for a well-earned rest. After the kitchen was cleaned and properly inspected, he and Thomas joined them. "Mrs. Cooper, I know how you feel about the military, but if you could spare the time, I would be forever grateful if you would have a long talk with my cook!" He was only half joking.

Rebecca accepted the compliment with the same quiet grace that the man had come to expect. "Thomas wrote some very funny letters about army cooking, Mr. Quinton. I couldn't have him coming home to sleep in the barn and eat hardtack! And I know him well enough to understand that he would not eat home cooking while everyone else ate army rations." She was happy that the men had had their own eating utensils and dishes, their mess kits."

Quinton exhaled. "Well, God bless Thomas!" He reconsidered. "And you, Mrs. Cooper. May God bless you."

Elizabeth and Naomi were asleep in their mother's lap. She hugged them both. "He already has, Mr. Quinton." Whispering, she called out to Thomas and Sally. "Can you help me with the girls?"

Thomas nodded, welcoming the opportunity. "I'll have to make a trade," he said softly. He was holding Sally's baby.

Carefully, Rebecca reached up and out, taking the sleeping child. "And then you and Sally can have some tea in the kitchen?" she suggested. Thomas nodded. He picked up Elizabeth, stepping back so that Sally could take Naomi.

Quinton waited to speak until the others had left the room. "Is she Thomas's woman?" he asked. It was not idle conversation and perhaps a bit forward but he felt a need to ask.

Rebecca considered before answering, and then asked a question of her own. "And why would that matter to thee?"

The young man thought for a long moment and then decided to be just as direct as the woman. "The men who are serving with me now — boys, some of them — are soldiers who have no families, no ties to any families I know of." He was quiet again, working the thing over in his mind. "If she is Thomas's woman and they have a child …" His words faded off into nothingness.

The fireplace was burning nicely now, the warm glow of yellow-tipped flames casting long shadows against the walls. Rebecca studied the young man's profile, unsure of what he was attempting to say, unsure of what he wanted her to say. "They all have families, Major Quinton, some-where and you need to remember that." The words came softly, carefully measured. She decided then not to go on with what she was thinking, choosing instead to simply answer his question. "Sally came to us like Thomas did, as a runaway. She was already with child and I didn't think it was safe for her to travel until after the child was born.

"I think Thomas cares for her. I think he is genuinely trying to feel something for the child. But they are not …"

Quinton interrupted without meaning to, thinking aloud. "… living together as man and wife." He was instantly ashamed that he could even suggest that this woman would have allowed two people who were not married to share a bed under her roof. Embarrassed at having been so forward, he stood up, eager to change the subject. "He could have a very good career in the military, Mrs. Cooper."

Rebecca rose up from her chair and went to the fireplace. She was still holding the sleeping infant and shifted the child to one arm as she tended the fire. Using the poker, she jabbed at the larger log that lay in the middle of the grate, finally turning it over. "He will have a better life here." She turned, facing the man. "I lost my son to your war, Major Quinton and my husband to that undeclared war called the Underground Railroad. I have no intention of losing Thomas to the Army."

The woman excused herself, brushing by the younger man. By the time she reached the door to the hallway she recanted somewhat and turned back. "In the end, Major Quinton, it will be Thomas's choice. Not yours and not mine. All I can do is pray that the War ends before any more young men die, on either side."

Quinton bowed politely, knowing their conversation was over. "Amen, Mrs. Cooper. Amen."

***

Thomas was on the hillside, his hand on the white picket fence he and the girls had placed around Jonathan's grave the previous summer. He stood there, studying the long shadow he cast across the snow-covered mound.

"Thee has come to say goodbye." Rebecca was beside him now and there were two shadows in the snow.

"Yes," Thomas reached up, taking off his cap. He put his arm around the woman's shoulder, pulling the cloak up around her neck.

"It's been a busy time for thee, Thomas," the woman smiled, "and an adventure."

He loved it when she said his name, the sound of it when she called to him or scolded him. Then, remembering where he was, he turned back to the grave, the two graves. Jonathan Cooper and his son were here, together. They would always be together. "What was he like?" He nodded toward the older grave, the lesser mound that had compacted with time.

"Little Jonathan," the woman breathed. It had been a long time since she had talked about her son. "Very much like his father," she said finally. Then, reconsidering, "Very much like Elizabeth." She thought of her mischievous daughter, the bright sparkle that all too often lit her summer-blue eyes.

"He was so young," Thomas breathed.

"He would have been nineteen this coming spring," the woman answered. She bent down, picking up a dead leaf from atop the snow. *Life is like this,* she thought, crumbling the leaf and scattering it before the wind, fragile and at the whim of man and nature. *Temporary.* She felt the old melancholia gripping her again and shrugged it off.

"You're cold," Thomas said. He took her arm, leading her back down the hill toward the house.

Rebecca paused her hand on the boy's arm. So much had happened in the last few days. Orders had arrived by dispatch for Major Quinton, directing him to the nearest railroad and then south for deployment. They would be going into the thick of it, moving at the forefront of a steadily growing Union force intended to push the Rebels out of the North. "Are thee sure, Thomas?" she asked. This very morning, when they were having their last cup of coffee, she — in her desperation and conviction that this war was wrong — had offered to buy him out of the Army, to pay his bounty. And she felt no guilt.

Thomas nodded. "Jonathan told me once — and so did Mr. Outerbridge — that if a thing is worth having, it's worth defending." The pair started walking again, crunching through the thawing ice and denting the snow. "I intend to come back, Rebecca. If it's all right with you, I intend to come back."

The woman nodded. "This is thy home, Thomas, for as long as thee needs and wants it."

The others were on the front porch, huddled together, Sally, Elizabeth and Naomi. They were waiting to say their goodbyes as well. Thomas opened his arms as he came up the stairs, pulling Sally to him. She buried her head against his shoulder. "You promised you wouldn't cry," the young man scolded. He smiled down at her. "I'll expect letters," he said, "Long letters." The girl nodded.

Elizabeth was more forward. She tugged at Thomas's sleeve. "I don't want you to go," she said, her chin jutting out.

Thomas bent down, hugging her. "I'll be back, Elizabeth. When this is over, I'll be back. I promise."

Naomi said nothing. She rushed the youth, her arms tight around his neck, her head hidden in his heavy coat. He pulled her away, feeling a lump in his throat. Of all of them, Naomi took things the hardest. He tugged at her pigtail, coaxing a smile and then stood up. Rebecca was still at his elbow. He took her arm. "Walk with me a way," he asked.

The woman nodded. She went with him, down the stairs, walking with him to the gate. "God go with thee, Thomas," she whispered when they reached the fence.

Thomas hugged her, aware of the men in the roadway

and the way they were watching him. It didn't matter. Then, turning smartly, he stared up at the young Major and saluted. "By your leave, sir."

Quinton returned the salute. "Sergeant Cooper." He watched as the young man moved to the head of the column and gave the order to move out. Then, turning slightly, he faced the woman. "Mrs. Cooper." The salute was prolonged and given with the deepest respect.

Rebecca watched after them, her gaze fastened on Thomas as he marched away. He cut a fine, proud figure in his blue uniform, a far cry from the starving wraith that had appeared in the loft of her barn so long ago.

It was a strange thing for the woman, the sense of pride that swelled within her. She had resigned herself to the young man's choice, his decision to yield to Frederick Douglass' entreaties to all the young, free blacks he had asked to serve. She thought again of Thomas's words, *if a thing is worth having, it's worth defending.* "God go with thee, Thomas." This time it was a prayer.

The young man had stopped at the rise in the road leading away from the farm. He paused and turned, lifting his hand in a final wave, his eyes taking in the panorama that spread below him. For the first time in his life, he was leaving a place that he regretted leaving, a place that he could hold in his heart.

A home. *His home.*

There was a determination in his step now and a deep sense of pride. He was free, truly free. Free to dream, free to choose.

He chose to fight.

A Look At: Long Ride To Limbo

GOLD, GOD AND GLORY.

Hernando Cortez had lived his life and the glory had been his. God watched over his deathbed and the gold...its secret soon to be buried with him...

Ten years earlier, Reese Sullivan rode away from his wife, Vanessa, and young son, Trey. Now they will embark on a perilous journey that pits father and son against unseen enemies, natural disaster, and each other—while back home the women they love face an unimagined danger.

Will they uncover the key to a vast and fabled treasure?

AVAILABLE NOW

About the Author

Kit Prate has always been a fan of Western fiction, but also tends towards anything on the written page that strikes her fancy.

Kit grew up as a curious child in a world of curiosity; blessed with parents who shared their sense of wonder in the small things, and a dry, mid-western sense of humor.

Luckily, marriage and work provided an opportunity to travel all across the US and into Mexico. That made it "easy" to write about places she'd seen and people she was fortunate to meet along the way.

Like a lot of authors, Kit Prate wants to try it all; although preferring the past to contemporary times. Happy endings? Maybe. Skewed logic and complex and conflicted characters, you bet. The world is an interesting place in fascinating shades of grey; not simply black and white.

www.ingramcontent.com/pod-product-compliance
Lightning Source LLC
Chambersburg PA
CBHW011456170626
46814CB00009B/3069